Red Sand

By T. S. Stribling

New York
Harcourt, Brace and Company

PRINTED IN THE U. S. A. BY
THE QUINN & BODEN COMPANY
RAHWAY, N. J.

CHES-CHA-MAY Book Club

	Rec.	Del.
Mrs.W.H.Mallory 1205 Union Ave.	Feb 15 — Mar 2	
Mrs. L.B.McFarland 1203 Union Ave.		
Mrs.Evander Williams 787 Jefferson Ave.		
Mrs.C.H.Grosvenor 579 Vance Ave.		
Mrs. Enoch Ensley 1573 Vinton Ave.	Oct.28 - Nov. 10	
Mrs. Martin Condon 1440 Central Ave.	Nov 11 "	
Mrs.Malcolm Semmee 1532 Poplar Ave.	Nov 25 "	
Mrs.Robt.T.Cooper 243 N.Montgomery St.	Dec 9. Dec 23	
rs.J.H.Falls 3 N.Bellevue St.	Dec 23. Jan 6	
rs.Thos.Day 1520 Central Ave.	Feb	
Miss Louise Looney 1584 Peabody Ave.	Jan 20 Feb 3	
Mrs.R.H.Vance 695 Melrose St.	Feb 7 " 13	

Keep two weeks and deliver to next on list

Red Sand

RED SAND

Chapter 1

On the west side of Candelaria Plaza which lies in the eastern purlieus of Caracas, Venezuela, there squats an old wineshop owned by one Pamba Malestar. This shop and its owner exert rather a large influence in instating the great, or at least the famous, in Venezuela. To mention a few of the *diestros* who have emerged from this old wine-scented chrysalis into fame, there are Rosalito, Conchito, Juanito, and so on "ito" after "ito," to say nothing of Lubito, who wielded his rapier to such an effect that he captured for himself in the Orinoco region a dictatorship about the size of England, Belgium, and France lumped together.

The inside of Señor Malestar's shop is cool and gloomy, and, of course, properly dusty, as all wine-shops should be, in order that any beam of light straying out of the *patio* into the interior must pick out a bloom of dust on ancient bottles before it flares up in their ruby or amber hearts.

5

A multiplicity of old tables, both square and round and blackened by years and liquor stains, are spaced among the square brick pillars which support the ceiling; and time and custom have divided the territory of the tables into very distinct sections, the coolest being reserved for the old Venezuelans, rich or poor, whose lifelong interest in, fidelity to, and unceasing conversation about, the great art of tauromachy entitles them to a seat among the doctors. The second most honorable position is over near the *patio* where the sippers of glasses can look out on a dilapidated pavement of red brick, at a great flare of bougainvillæa which rides the wall in a purple curve and among whose profusion of blooms a tropical butterfly occasionally wanders, and, in very rare instances, flickers down on the very wine glasses themselves, unrolls its long tube and drinks with the *toreros*, to their health no doubt. For this space of tables is reserved for the *diestros*, the *espadas*, and the *banderilleros*, the attendants of the bull ring. No one ever questioned the right of these men of the *circo* to seats giving on the *patio* with its sweet flowers and sunshine and jeweled lizards and butterflies. It was highly fit that these men should absorb while they could the movement and color and sweetness of life; they, whose own lives, one day,

would most probably flicker out, pinned to the sand
by a bull's horn while ten thousand crazy spectators
banked in the oval gasp and shriek.

The remainder of that expanse of tables is given
over to the *gente*, that is to say, the mob, the *hoi
polloi*, the sons and daughters of nobody.

On this particular afternoon a certain stir in the
wineshop was occasioned by old Malestar pasting a
new folder against the dusty mirror of his bar and
laying a few more on his counter at the hands of
his patrons. A group of dignified and leathery old
gentlemen in the remote and coolest part of the
house immediately beckoned a *criado* to fetch some
of the folders. Soon their endless gossip took on an
explosive quality. They leaned over the tables and
stressed their words with clenched fists. One of
them hissed: "But, Señor, he breaks all precedents,
Juan Leon! Why not Leonito? Has he no consideration for the lungs of the spectators! How can
one shout Juan Leon! Juan Leon! Impossible!"

"But, no, Señor, it is the new style in Spain; dignity, simplicity. Why call himself 'Little John,'
or 'Little Lion,' *Cá*, why not simply John Lion?"

"But that is not his real name!"

"Quien sabe?"

Another one thumped on the folder and disputed the printed text: "How can his cape play be more perfect than that of Orlandito—that *hombre* was a shadow, incomparable. I tell you I saw him get the *cogida* that killed him . . ."

"And he perfect?" interposed a third voice ironically.

"The bull made a false charge."

"A thoroughbred Spanish fighting bull made a false charge!"

A pause, then a shrug, a spreading of the hands: "They say he beat his wife unduly, Señor. He was an artist, you know, and had temperament, and I have always thought it was the finger of Him Who Moves Us All reached down into the *circo* and La! An impossibility! A Spanish fighting bull charges falsely! A wife is avenged. . . . Say what you will, Señors, such an interposition was not lost on Guillermo Sandoval. I have been more regular at the masses since I saw Orlandito go down."

A moment of reverent silence followed this confession of faith, then a practical voice said: "We would all better see Malestar and reserve our seats now. *Caramba!* Juan Leon and his fighting bulls —the *circo* will be packed!"

Several of the old men nodded meditatively;

others sipped their wine; others looked dreamily at old Malestar far across the wineshop behind his bar. Yes, decidedly, seats must be procured without a moment's delay. All agreed to that, and they drifted into their endless gossip again.

Over near the *patio* silhouetted against the purple bougainvillæa sat a youth of powerful mold and rather handsome brunet features. He, too, sat perusing the new poster on the filmed mirror over the bar and he compared it in growing displeasure with an old hand sheet which had been stuck there for a long time. The athletic young man read the new placard slowly, his lips fashioning each word without sound after the manner of semi-literate folk:

"Señor Morear touring the South American Capitols with a herd of Spanish fighting bulls wishes to present to the citizens of Caracas

JUAN LEON

Premier *Espada* of the Imperial Circo in Madrid, at NUEVO CIRCO on Agosto Fifteenth, 1924. Six Spanish Bulls will be used.

Admission Bs.100. Bs.60. Bs.40. Bs.20. Reservations now on sale."

Then followed press notices from the sporting papers of Madrid, Cordova, Seville, Barcelona. These were limited to catch phrases followed by the signature of the paper:

"Fulfilment of art," "a continuous picture, graceful as sculpture, flexible as scandal," "Juan Leon, who has translated the prose of bullfighting into the poetry of tauromachy," and so on for half a dozen ingeniously turned paragraphs.

The old poster which had been stuck on the mirror for a long time was an evilly printed sheet in two colors and it represented a man with a brilliant red cape standing the charge of a huge red and black bull which blew red streams from its nostrils. Above and below this picture was displayed the following text:

Angelito!   Angelito!   Angelito!

The Unspeakable; the Incomparable, the Supernal! Will Kill Seven Ferocious Bulls in Nuevo Circo Sunday Afternoon at Two O'clock. A Thrilling Exhibition of the Most Reckless Courage and the Most Consummate Skill. Do not Fail to See the Daredevil Angelito.

Angelito!   Angelito!   Angelito!

Admission Bs.3. Bs.2.50. Bs.2. Bs.1.

There were no press notices. Now there had been a time when that villainous poster struck a chord of music in the broad breast of the young man who perused it, but to-day, in juxtaposition with the new notice, there was something very wrong with it. The athlete hardly knew what. He stared at it with pained eyes, moving his lips to the familiar words, but he could not for his life put his finger precisely on the weakness which he felt to be there.

"Now by San Pablo," he thought gloomily, "that is a strange thing. Here this Juan Leon has no big words, no red type, no exclamation points and yet somehow . . . somehow . . ."

He tapped his fingers on the table utterly puzzled as to how the Spanish poster obtained its effect of dignity and sincerity which his own so signally lacked. For naturally the young man who sat tattooing on the table top was Angelito! Angelito! Angelito! billeted to kill seven ferocious bulls in Nuevo Circo on Sunday afternoon at two o'clock. The reason the old poster set no date for this daredevil feat was because Angelito performed it every Sunday afternoon at two o'clock.

As Angelito criticized his own placard there entered the wineshop one of those slender, handsome,

and somewhat melancholy looking young Venezuelans such as lounge in every club in Caracas.
This one loitered into the door, glanced over the
interior, and presently threaded his way toward the
section reserved for bullfighters with an air of one
possessing an immense but saddened leisure. He
smiled faintly at the *torero* as he came up and a
moment later leaned over him in a perfunctory embrace; then he slipped into a chair on the other side
of the table with a slight shrug and a down-drawing
of his handsome red lips which meant that after all
he and the bullfighter might as well go on living,
there being little else to do.

After the usual polite fencing with *"buenos
diases"* and an inquiring about their respective
health, the *torero*, using the intimate Spanish *"tu"*
asked, "Have you read the notice of the coming
circo, Rafael?"

Rafael wagged a negative finger and using the
formal *"usted,"* "Kind of you to mention it, but that
no longer interests me, Angelito."

The bullfighter stared: "What? Not interested
in the Spanish *circo?"*

"Alas! . . . no." He held up both palms and
dropped them.

"But why? *Mi cara amigo!"*

"I cannot speak of it, my dear Angelito."

"*Pobrecito!* What has happened?"

"You know my mother had always forbid my spreading a cape before a bull, even a young bull."

"*Si,*" admitted Angelito with a little shrug, "but you have always done it when you liked."

"Certainly, but the treacherousness of women! Ah, Angelito!"

"What have they done now?" asked the bull-fighter in amazement.

"What should my *madre* do," cried Rafael, "but go to my *inamorata,* the exquisite Señorita Margherita Miraflores and together they plan this *coup.* I am not even to fight young bulls! I am tied, pinioned, bound by my word as a *caballero!*"

"*Por l'amor de Dios!*" cried Angelito. "How did they do it?"

"Wait! Stay!" cried Rafael. "I have here a little verse that says it better than I can. I spent all last night composing it after I came back from the window of the Señorita Miraflores. I call it, "*Espada, Adios!*" (Rapier, Farewell.)

With a trembling hand the young man drew from an inner pocket a sheet of parchment rolled in silk. The mere unrolling perfumed the air about the table. When it was discovered there appeared on the sheepskin a poem engrossed with rubric capitals in the most painstaking manner.

Rafael leaned across the table, poised his right hand to be ready for his gestures and said, "Listen:

ESPADA, ADIOS

'The night was yearning, tumultuous,
And I could not discern in my passion
The breath of the sad *frangipanni*
From the maddening scent of her tresses,
Implacable, insolent tresses
That coil as an aspic Colubrian
Benumbing the will and the vigor
And the masculine surge of the heartbeat.

'I forswore what was highest within me,
The flare of the yellow arena,
The lunge of black lethal horns
And the delicate crimson cloak play
That wafts aside death, enigmatic.

'Oh, *Espada,* the Cristo of Spaniards,
Whose hilt is a cross and is sacred!
Oh, could I forget and forswear thee,
Bound in a pair of weak arms
To the jealous bars of her window;
Ensnared in a coil of curls,
Of aspic, Colubrian tresses.

'But I will awake from the spell
Oh, *Espada,* the Cristo of Spaniards,
I will awake and will see
For what I have bartered thy slimness;
The padre will break down the bars
With a mumbling of words and a blessing,
And *crac!* Then I will awake
To a fat wife and four squalling babies!' "

At this point Rafael flung down his poem and broke into ironic laughter. "I don't understand it!" he cried. "By San Pedro, it escapes me!"

The bullfighter stared at his friend blankly. "Neither do I. What does it mean?"

"What does what mean?"

"*Pues,* the poem."

Rafael became gloomily sober again. "*Cá!* The poem. Oh, that means that my mother and sister went to the Señorita Miraflores and persuaded her to make me promise never to fight another bull, that's what the poem means."

"Did you promise it?"

"*Sangre de Cristo, hombre,* of course I promised it!"

The bullfighter and his friend sat silent in the face of this calamity. Angelito looked out into the *patio* and watched a green lizard make a dart across the red brick pavement, then stop amid flight to jiggle up and down on its tiny forelegs after the absurd manner of its kind.

A shuffling near his table caused him to glance around and he saw old Malestar approaching. The old fellow was nut brown, wrinkled and humped. He wore nothing on his feet except the *alpargatas* of a peon, although he owned the famous wineshop, was the impresario and dictator of all the bullfights in Venezuela, and must have been a millionaire, in *bolivars* at least.

Now he came up rubbing his hands exactly like an ordinary waiter saying: "I hope you like your drinks, Señors, *beber es vivir*" (to drink is to live), and he chuckled over the worn Spanish; then he added, "Señor Angelito, may I drop a word in your ear?"

Rafael immediately arose, "I was just going, *tío* (uncle), if you will pardon me, Angelito . . ." He was about to bow himself away.

The bullfighter was annoyed out of his gloss of suavity. He made a rough peon gesture and said: "No, stay where you are, Rafael—*Tío* Malestar, we are *amigos*. You may say anything before my friend, Rafael!"

Rafael's oval olive face betrayed the faintest surprise at this outburst, but he lingered a moment evidently a little undecided what to do. The old wine seller took a second glance at Angelito to make sure he was not tipsy, then with a little gesture of complaisance, said: "It is a slight thing, Señors; I have just received a telegram from the *alcalde* of Valencia asking for a *quadrillo*. He makes a fiesta to-morrow in honor of San Blas and he desires a bullfight. The fight will take place directly after High Mass, so if any fighter cares to accept the purse, he may return on the afternoon train, God willing." The old man crossed himself.

At this announcement the bullfighter was immediately sorry he had not allowed Rafael to depart. He wanted to ask the size of the purse, but that was impossible before a member of the wealthy Jiminez family.

Old Malestar had foreseen this difficulty and now he cleared his throat and said: "It is a great fiesta, Señor; the Bishop himself is going to administer the holy sacrament to a class of novices and naturally they desire a very sharp and bloody *corrida*. There will be much er . . . er . . . fame."

The *torero* was so uncomfortable before Rafael that he did not understand this substitution of "fame" for "money." He was about to reject the offer when Rafael leaned across the table. "Take it," he counseled briefly.

"Why?" cried Angelito a little alarmed for fear that Rafael thought he was poor and needed the purse whatever it was.

"Because," explained Rafael, with a brilliancy coming into his handsome face, "I am going with you as second *espada*."

Both the old man and the bullfighter stared at this youth, who, both knew, had never fought anything except young bulls in his life.

"*Por Dios*, Señor Jiminez," cried old Malestar with horror in his face, "it's impossible! A Jiminez fighting in a public *corrida!*"

"I will not fight as a Jiminez, I will go unknown." He gave this last word a romantic intonation.

"But the purse is nothing," cried the shopkeeper, seizing this chance to interpolate the information, "a paltry fifteen hundred bolivars" ($300.00).

The *novillero* made a gesture which expressed disdain of the purse. "Keep that for yourself, *tío*."

Old Malestar was visibly overcome. "*Demonio*, what a man!"

Angelito was ashamed of the old peon's outburst over money; it somehow reflected on his own generosity.

"But, Rafael," expostulated the bullfighter, "you have given your fiancée your word as a *caballero. . . .*"

The young man shrugged politely as if arguing with the girl herself. "I will fight under a pseudonym, and besides, she will never know it."

"But you promised her. You pledged yourself as a Jiminez . . ."

Rafael turned in amazement on his friend: "*Sangre de Cristo!* The promises a man makes to a woman are for her peace of mind, Angelito. They are made to comfort her, to protect her. They are expressions of immediate love and tenderness, not maps of future conduct!"

"God listen to you!" exclaimed Angelito who had never had occasion to take this aristocratic view of pledges to women.

"*Seguro,*" continued Rafael, turning to the old man, "I did give my promise, *Tío* Malestar, and it was a bitter renunciation." Rafael became grave at the recollection. "I think I may say, *tío,* it caused me more pain than I have felt since the burial of my father, God rest his soul." The three men crossed themselves reverently. "To give up my sword, the color of my life, my slender virgin of death! Ah, *tío,* that was a great pain!"

"Caramba, si," hissed the wine seller impressed.

"But, *tio,* like all great sorrows it reacted on my heart, and if I may say it, inspired one of my loftiest songs. Here, listen, I call it, *'Espada, Adios!'* . . ."

Rafael drew the old peon toward him nervously, got out his parchment, unrolled the silk. As the perfume floated into air once more old Uncle Malestar sniffed noisily, blinked his eyes and stuck out his tongue at Angelito to denote satisfaction in the odor.

The bullfighter grew hot under his sallow skin. Such grossness in the old peon in some mysterious way redounded on himself. He thought with savagery, "God's lightning strike this old monkey!"

By this time Rafael was well launched on his poem, reading it dramatically. Old Malestar picked up the manuscript cover from the table, pressed it to his wide nostrils and stood inhaling, and presumably listening, with his eyes shut.

The reading over, old Malestar shook hands effusively with the poet. As the two young men prepared to go, young Jiminez said he would be forced to beg a favor of Angelito. He wanted the bullfighter to go to the Jiminez villa and fetch his rapier, cloak, brocaded jacket, sash, and trousers. "Because," he explained, "if my sister and mother so much as see me lift the corner of my cape, they begin weeping and warning and begging and I have really a devil of a time."

"Will they give them to me to bring to you?"

"Tell them you are a *novillado,* and I am lending you my things for a try out. I'll give you a note." Rafael stopped outside the wineshop, produced a memorandum book and a gold magazine pencil and scribbled a sheet. "That will do it. Just drive around with all my things to your own *casa* and we will start from there in the morning."

The *torero* took the note with a certain pleasure in being dispatched in this intimate fashion to the Jiminez villa. He hailed a cab, got in and the two friends waved *adios* at each other as Angelito drove off.

The swaying of the cab over the cobblestones was grateful to the *torero*. As a Latin he had a child-like enjoyment of his immediate physical pleasures. Now and then, he saw the cabman above him lift a hand to his cap. By this Angelito knew they were passing a church and he mechanically touched the brim of his own expensive hat.

Presently he began planning what he would say when he reached the Jiminez villa. He drew out a case of cork-tipped cigarettes, lighted one thought-

fully, looked at the end to see if it were burning
evenly; he would say, "Pardon me, Señorita, for intruding on your charming leisure, . . ." It really
seemed quite graceful and easy; of course, some of
the effect would depend on how he said it.

Paraiso is in Caracas what the Gold Coast is in
Chicago, and Fifth Avenue is in New York; except
in Paraiso all the villas are surrounded by grounds
which look as green and exotic as hothouses. The
buildings themselves are painted in the brightest of
blues and yellows and greens to keep in tone with
the quiver of sunshine amid palms, bamboos, ban-
yans, and the shrill red of the poinsettias.

Angelito got out of his cab and told the driver to
wait. The stone pillars of the Jiminez gate and the
tall iron bars of the fence imposed themselves on
the *torero*. He was not accustomed to ornamental
grounds. In fact, except in Paraiso, all the houses
of Caracas are built solidly together along the *calles*,
and now these enclosures, lush with greenery
breathed an opulence that was strange to the bullfighter. He thought over his sentence a little dubiously, "intruding on your charming leisure . . ."

He moistened his red lips as he opened the great
gate with its iron bars pointing like spears to heaven.

It seemed rather a long walk from the gate to the front door of the villa. Once there he pressed the button and got out his note hurriedly. Then he stood staring at the door, holding his note in readiness, like a delivery boy.

He had to ring three times and stood in a curious suspense when he heard a shuffling inside, and a mulatto maid opened the door. Angelito was greatly relieved to see that it was the maid who answered the door and he handed her the note in silence.

The girl looked up, evidently decided some point in her mind in the bullfighter's favor, for she dealt him a deliberate little blow with her black eyes, followed this with a brief but intimate smile, then took the note with an air that showed the note in no wise pertained to them, that it was merely something they passed along to high, but rather nebulous ends, and that he, the messenger, and she, the maid, were the real sap and substance of life and all this folderol of notes and calls and society didn't amount to a dried mango seed. She took the note, touching his hand momentarily with her rough fingers and disappeared without a word.

Angelito stood smiling, perfectly at ease and expecting the maid to return lugging Rafael's fighting outfit. After a wait there came a noise inside which might possibly have been the maid returning and dragging the cloak along the floor. The door opened and Angelito's courage sank when he saw a *señora* and two *señoritas* in the entrance inspecting him.

The *señora,* a large, exceedingly handsome woman with a faint mustache asked in a baritone voice, "Who wants these things, Señor?"

Angelito moistened his red lips, "I do, Señora."

The smaller *señorita* in some sort of purple silk gown loosed a cascade of impatient Spanish.

"Ciertamente! We know you do, Señor, but to whom are you going to take it?" She used the familiar *"tu"* with which Venezuelans address inferiors.

"I—I—I am going to use it myself, Señorita."

"You, a *novillero?"* whipped out the girl incredulously.

"But, Margherita," interposed the pleasant voice of the taller *señorita,* "look at his shoulders!"

"Caramba, all men have shoulders, Socorro!"

"But—ah—all of him, Margherita. It may be that Rafael thinks this *joven* has talent and that he will make a *diestro* one day."

"I'm sure he chooses odd friends," whipped out Margherita.

The *señora* with the baritone voice interposed to

say, "That man can't get on Rafael's jacket or pantaloons either."

The girl called Socorro laughed in a pleasant way, *"Anda, madre,* that is their look-out. And think if Rafael should develop some one into a bull-fighter, that would be something."

These repeated suggestions that some day he might make a bullfighter piqued Angelito. He fumed within himself.

"Diantre, they don't know I am Angelito! This blobby old *mujer* and these soft *señoritas* come and shriek themselves hoarse over me every Sunday afternoon, throw me handkerchiefs, jewelry, purses, and the devil knows what, and now when they meet me, they stare at me and think I may make a *torero,* that there is a chance that I will make a *torero—* *Huy!"*

Under the force of his disgust, a sudden and odd revenge popped into Angelito's head. He made a low bow and said, "Pardon me, Señora, Señoritas, for intruding on your charming leisure, but if I should rip Rafael's jacket I would certainly have it stitched back very carefully."

"Oh, you needn't mind that," interposed the baritone, rather ashamed of her inhospitality. But Angelito went on suavely: "And I trust you will allow

me to return your pocket handkerchief, Señorita."
He reached in his pocket, fished out a bit of lace
and cambric, bowed again and presented it to the
girl Socorro.

This *señorita* took the handkerchief in some surprise and looked at it, "Why this is my handkerchief!"

"*Seguro,* Señorita."

She looked up at the *torero,* "Where did you get
it?"

"You let it drop, Señorita."

"I—" She looked about her, "Did I drop my
handkerchief?"

The smaller girl said, "Is it really your handkerchief?" and took it from her.

"Señor," asked the baritone, "where did you get
this handkerchief?"

Angelito thought quickly. "I picked it up on the
sand, Señora." He glanced down at the sanded
walk.

"Ah, here in the front door," said the baritone.
"You are careless, Socorro." She turned inside the
hall, "You may bring Rafael's things, Lizetta."

The mulatto girl appeared with the *novillero's*
equipment. This time she had the expressionless

face of a servant in the presence of her mistress. She hesitated a moment whether or not to give them directly to Angelito, but the bullfighter solved the problem by hailing the cabman. The fellow hustled down from his high seat and came running to take the bundle. The mere manner in which the cabman ran told the importance of his fare. It had its effect.

Angelito bowed to the ladies with the suppleness of his profession. He felt at a spiteful ease now. His eyes glittered maliciously at Socorro, *"Adios,* Señora, Señoritas," and he walked away.

The women in the doorway watched him. The Señorita Margherita said: "Socorro, he didn't find this handkerchief on the walk. It smells of cigarettes. He's had it in his pocket for a long time."

The dowager said in her deep voice, "Rafael picks such odd friends."

The girl Socorro stood studying the stranger who was carrying away Rafael's fighting things. She said half to herself and half to her companion, "If you think all men have shoulders like his, Margherita, you are not very observing."

Angelito returned to his vehicle, directed the cabby to the Matadero, and drove off with a flourish

and much self-satisfaction. He had come off very
well indeed he thought. As he spun along the fragrant boulevard of Paraiso his thoughts clung to
the *señoritas* he had just met. He could not remember how the tall one looked. He held simply an
impression of silks, a pensive oval face, a rather pale
complexion and splendid dark eyes. His prevailing
impression was that she was a very luxurious girl.
She was one of those *señoritas*, born and bred in
Paraiso, who flung him jewels and handkerchiefs on
Sunday afternoons, when, for her amusement, he
grazed injury by a hair, and who didn't know him
from the Cid on week days.

He peered out of his cab at the villas he was passing and he thought with a certain unhappiness that
these bright dwellings were full of beautiful
señoritas, all as far away from him as the moon.
It seemed to Angelito that they moved about on
some stratum high in the air and on Sunday afternoons they came to the edge of their clouds and
looked down on him in the bull ring and applauded
and laughed and cheered and then, straightway,
were drawn up again into some sort of heaven where
he could not follow them at all.

The cab turned out of the boulevard into a more
ordinary *calle;* the houses thickened and eventually

coalesced. Then he was trotting toward the Matadero through the scents and naked children and street venders of the slums. Paraiso had vanished from his sight and nostrils just as it must vanish from his life and vague desires.

After ten or twelve blocks the sewage-scented *calle* gave way to a sort of neglected ornamental ground set with tall Lombardy poplars. A street car track ran down through this ground, circled at the end and returned. Beyond the circling car track among the Lombards he saw a broad one-story structure of red brick flanked by numberless cattle pens. The moment his cab drew up to let him out he caught the rumor of a great disturbance in the pens; the bellowing of bulls, the shouting of men, the clatter of hoofs over stone pavements. Angelito walked briskly through the sunshine toward this place. The pungent and rather sickening smell of blood came to his nose.

All this was as familiar to the *torero* as the palm of his hand. From this place he had sprung. Amid this confusion of cattle and men he had started his own career as a *torero*. He recalled as distinctly as yesterday how he had walked, year after year, from the *adobe* tenements down the car track to the Matadero because he had not the *centisimos* to ride.

He remembered his thrill one day when he was chosen out of this bedlam to act as *monosabio* at the Viejo Circo; that was before the new *circo* had been built. He recalled just how proud he had been of his red shirt and blue trousers; how he had strutted about and handed the *banderillas* to the *banderilleros* and had helped chain the dead bulls for the mules to drag them out. For all this old Malestar had given him a silver *peso* and a bottle of sour wine. It had made him deliriously happy and inordinately rich. He had never been so happy or so wealthy again.

As Angelito walked to the broad brick building of the Matadero, he could see the top runners of the pens on the south side of the building lined with shouting and laughing boys and men. They were as thick as green parrots in a cashew tree, and as noisy. They were whooping and shrilling at innumerable bullfights which were taking place inside the pens. Now and then they leaped from their roost on the top of the fence and ran a few steps shouting with laughter. This was when a bull on the inside swerved toward their dangling legs. The moment the bull had passed they clambered back up to their ringside seats.

Occasionally through the legs of the onlookers,

Angelito could catch a glimpse of a bull charging a man in the pens and hear the huzzah of applause if the man stood his ground well and sidestepped narrowly.

That was the great idea in bullfighting, to elude the horns by as narrow a margin as one's nerves allowed. Once in a long while one of these peons at the Matadero was gored or killed.

Fastened over the door of the wide brick building was the head of a bull. The head was nailed there because the bull had accounted for one of the peons before it had died. The head was an epitaph to some *novillero's* rashness.

When Angelito opened the door and entered, confusion smote his senses; a bellowing and shouting in his ears, the smell of hot blood in his nostrils and a half a dozen bulls charging over the red concrete floor of the *abbatoir* at the butchers who waved red tow sacks at them and lured them to attack.

The animals, maddened by the odor, shouts and red sacks, lunged after the half-naked men with the greatest fury. The butchers poised themselves on the slippery floor until the last moment, then stepping to one side, let the bulls dash up their sacks. If an animal tried to wheel, its hoofs would slip on the bloody floor and it would thunder down and its jaws and knees would bang against the concrete. As it struggled to get up a man called a *puntillero* would rush to the animal, give it a swift jab with a *puntillo,* or sharp iron spike, on the top of its head just behind the horns. Through a tiny unprotected spot, the iron snipped the spinal column and the struggling bull collapsed as if struck by lightning. Immediately three or four peons ran to the dead bull, beheaded him, disemboweled him, flung his skin to one side, cut him into pieces and dragged the pieces along the nasty floor to tubs of dirty water where the raw beef was washed; then it was hung up on hooks along the walls.

While this was going on there played over the whole scene a constant shimmer of flies. The flies were like a dancing veil between bulls and men; they swarmed over the hides, the meat, the men, the bulls; every movement flushed a gauze of them and deposited them at another place. Charging bulls, dodging men, swarming flies, that was the Matadero, or government slaughter house, in Caracas. This was the kindergarten, prep, and high school of *toreros.* Four years before a barefooted, bare-bodied peon boy worked in this Gehenna. A *mono-sabio* had been required at the Viejo Circo, and he was given a chance. To-day that boy had driven down to the Matadero in a cab to select two more boys for *monosabios* and give them a chance. He wanted them to go with him to the coming bullfight in Valencia.

Chapter 2

NORTHWARD from Candelaria Plaza runs a *calle* composed of two solid rows of stuccoed houses and a cobbled pavement. It diminishes with distance until it reaches the sharp acclivity of the mountains on the North of Caracas and there the thoroughfare becomes a mule trail, and any one standing in the plaza still can see it, a very faint, broken, yellow line zig-zagging tediously up the vast, purple-gray massif.

The name of this *calle* and trail is Traposo, for once there was a trappist monastery in the mountains reached by this route. A little grass ventures to grow between the cobbles in Traposo *calle*, and it is rather thicker toward the middle because here it is watered and enriched by the sewage of all the houses in the street; for this waste flows on the surface and pursues an impartial course down the exact middle of the street.

One of the *casas* on this thoroughfare was stuccoed, painted a light blue with panels of a deeper blue and was decorated with shining bronze grills in front of doors and windows.

From across the street an old peon woman approached this *casa* as she shuffled back from morning mass at Candelaria church. She stopped at the bright grill before the door, drew a bunch of keys from under her skirt, unlocked it and swung it open for the day. Then she unlocked a small panel inset in the left shutter of the big double doors.

She stood for a moment in the weak light of the rising sun looking down on the city, which was covered by the morning mists. The mist lay in a level lake of the palest opalescence and concealed everything. The very *calle*, in which the old woman stood, marched down into it and was lost. At a little distance away, out of it, arose the two old towers of the Candelaria throwing bluish shadows on the pearly level lake.

Beyond these lovely architectural islets lay other towers and spires for a mile across and three or four miles long, like bouys marking a drowned city.

But the faëry quality of this scene was lost on the old peon woman. The only object which held her eyes in this sea of nacre was a huge circular mass some half a mile to the southward. This huge cylindrical structure with its battlemented top was so placed that its eastern half was gilded a bright red while its western moiety was lost in a deep blue.

Barely discernible against its mighty façade was the inscription, *"Sol y Sombra,"* or that is to say, "Sunshine and Shadow," but used on a bull ring it designates the division of the seats and corresponds with the English, "bleachers and grandstand." As if the distribution of light on the distant *circo* were symbolic, the *"sol"* on the eastern rhomb was brightly illuminated, while the *"sombra"* to the west faded into shadow.

The old crone stared at this heavy, colorful building against the sea of pearl, blinked her eyes, and at last lifted the edge of her old *mantilla* to wipe them. As she did so she whispered in the blurred Spanish of her sort, "Oh, *Madre de Dios,* what an ugly place! What a horrible place! Sweet Virgin, please send a *terremoto* and shake it down!" In the passion of her malediction, she crossed herself, kissed her thumb nail, and went inside.

The blue *casa* had a wide tiled hallway with rooms on the right hand or northern side. This passage led straight on back into a bare *patio* surrounded by a colonnade with pink twisted columns and elaborate capitals. In the center of the *patio* was a fountain which was dry because the old woman could not endure the expense of allowing it to run.

On both sides of the *patio* were rooms, and at one
of these doors the old woman knocked and called,
"Pancho! Pancho!" She paused a moment, then
flung out an aside: *"Caramba,* still in bed! Perhaps it is just as well he fights bulls. He would
never make an honest living! Pancho! Pancho!"
she croaked again.

Came the sound of a turning and groaning, then
a querulous voice asked, *"Madre,* how often have I
begged you never to call me Pancho again?"

"Oiga Jesu!" cried the old woman angrily.
"Denying the name the *padre* gave him when he
lay screaming against my breast! *Huy!* Anyway, get up! Your coffee is ready. You ought to
be married, Pancho, then you would have to get
up."

Came a silence, then the bullfighter said, "I am
thinking of getting a woman, *madre."*

The old woman in the mantilla stiffened, stared at
the door shutter. *"Diantre!* Who are you about
to bring here, Pancho?"

"Pues," strung out the man's voice quizzically,
"a peon girl."

The old woman exploded. "A peon girl! A peon!
Cá! The slut, the hussy! This is a fine catch of

fish; risking your life for a fine *casa* like this and then bringing a peon girl . . ."

The bullfighter laughed, "No, that was a joke, *madre;* I have in mind a very fine lady, a beautiful *señorita*, a—"

"*Sangre de Cristo!* You wear the head of a donkey, Pancho, for all your fine feathers! A fine lady! A beautiful *señorita!* Don't you know she will marry you just for your money!"

"No, but she is rich herself," said the son seriously, "much wealthier than I am."

"Rich! Rich! That makes it all the worse, Pancho! She will marry you to betray you! None of these fine ladies are true to their husbands! *Caramba!* Such a *bobo!* Only peon women are true to their men; at least many of them are—I was."

Angelito broke out laughing heartily at this outburst, then he caught himself up and reproved the crone. "Are you without shame, *madre?* No lady would speak of such things to her son!"

"*Cá!* I'm no lady, I'm an honest peon!"

"I say you are not a peon!" cried the bullfighter sharply. "Whoever heard of a peon living in such a *casa* as this, and lying in bed till—what is the hour?"

"It is eight and has a good way on nine."

"*Caramba!*" Came the sound of a swift springing out of bed and dressing.

At that moment the door bell rang and the *torero* called loudly, "See who is at the door, Ana!"

The old woman instantly dropped her rôle of mother and became a servant, shuffling toward the entrance. In the hallway she called, "Who is it, in the name of Christ?"

And from outside the portals came the response in carefully enunciated Spanish, "We come in peace, the Señors Jiminez and Montauban."

The old woman became agitated. She went flying to the doors and unbolted both big shutters. Under her breath she was gasping, "Holy Mary, a Jiminez and a Montauban! Next my son will have down the bishop himself!" and she threw both big portals open as if she were admitting a regiment.

The good woman attempted to induct her visitors into a wonderful salon, the first room on the right. She held open its door and displayed a gloomy interior with a pair of crossed rapiers and some religious lithographs on the wall. But the two men, who were under the impression that they were in bachelors' quarters, said they would shout Angelito out of his room.

The bullfighter himself heard their voices and called through the panel that he would be out in a moment and that they must have a cup of coffee before they started.

The two visitors protested, but their host called out, "Ana, coffee for the *caballeros!*" and the next moment he flung his shutter open and appeared in the doorway.

"Señors," he cried, "my *casa* and all that it holds is yours!" He came out with a hand extended to each guest. "Take my left hand, Señor Montauban, it is nearest my heart," he welcomed.

The old peon woman, who was hurrying through the *patio* to the kitchen in the rear, paused to look back at this cavalier reception and nod her head in pleasure.

"Angelito," said Señor Montauban, taking the *toreros's* hand in both his own, "I have just been remonstrating with Rafael on the folly of going to Valencia on such an adventure . . ."

The *torero* looked at young Jiminez, "If Rafael doesn't want to go I can easily find another *espada* . . ."

"*Caramba,* but I do want to go!" cried Rafael.

"But I say it is a mad hazard!" protested Montauban.

"It is one Angelito accepts every Sunday, Narciso."

"That is quite beside the point, *mi caro amigo*. Angelito has been drilled in the fundamentals of bullfighting. He had the broadest foundation. In his youth he voluntarily surrendered the pleasures of most young men and stayed in the Matadero from morning till night studying bulls, learning to read the bovine mind. He is a ripened *diestro*, while you, pardon my frankness, you have fought young bulls perhaps twenty times in your life."

"*Valgame Dios*, I think my sister has turned you into an old maid!"

Montauban flushed somewhat beneath his sallow skin, "No, I simply dislike to see a dear friend . . . "

"Every one fights his first bull at some time, Narciso, and what a night I have spent with this *corrida* in prospect! *Caramba*, the stars never shone so sweetly, Narciso. I thought, 'perhaps these are the last stars I will ever see.' I held out my arms to them and tried to think, 'never to see the stars again, never; let me gaze my last time on the stars.'"

The two men were looking at the poet half serious and half smiling. "Rafael," said Montauban, "sometimes I think you are mad."

Young Jiminez broke out laughing. "You your-self, Narciso, in your paper advise men to live each day as though it were their last. You promulgate the doctrine that this is the only way in which we can feel the warmth and uniqueness of life."

"I stand to it," hesitated Montauban. "It is a mood to assume. But I had no intention to suggest to a dear friend, whom I aspire to make my brother-in-law, to risk his life . . ."

"Ah, there you are!" cried the poet earnestly. "That is the secret malady of all Venezuelans, the impulse to sit and fancy this or that and to attempt nothing. They never reach the real ictus in the prosody of life, action. Unless a man place his life at a real hazard, Narciso, he cannot possibly feel the ecstasy of living. God's lightning! How my pulse leaped when I awoke this morning! Be sure I got up betimes to see the sunrise. The first I have seen in years, and I thought, but wait—one moment—" As he uttered these words in his excited voice, he drew from his pocket a parchment, un-rolled it, and began to read:

"If this be my last,
　Let me bare my breast to its creeping gold,
　Let me clasp the sun in my arms and drink
　　its light to the last drop.

I will absorb it all, the sun, the mountains,
    level lake of pearl,
Cathedral towers like curious carven isles,
And swallows dipping to the misty sea.

"This moment I am they,
    Their mystic whole somehow dissolved in
      me;
Each disparate part knows not itself; nor
    whole, the aching beauty of the whole.
Without me, all were chaos.

"Therefore, O black horned bull,
    Knock not too roughly at a *torero's* breast
With keen inquisitive horns, lest thy rash
    fury
Shatter sunrise, light and fragrance,
Swallows dipping to a misty sea, and
    plunge all into endless and untimely
    night."

Señor Montauban suddenly threw his arms about
the poet.

"Rafael!" he cried. "What perfection!" He held
his friend off by the shoulder to look at him, "May
Heaven strike me if I allow such a genius to be ex-
posed in the bull ring—what do you call it?"

"A Premonition of Night," said Rafael warming
to his friend's praise.

"*Caramba,* what a splendid paradox, to describe a sunrise and involve in it the coming of night."

"There you are," cried Rafael delighted, "I did not have to study and beat my head to produce that fancy. *Pues,* it was forced on me. When a man sees a sunrise which may very well be his last, *naturalmente,* he thinks of the night."

Señor Montauban looked at his friend, spread his hands hopelessly, "*Ola,* what an exquisite instrument to be battered around a bull ring—but at any rate, Rafael, you must give me the verses to print in '*Sol y Sombra.*'"

Rafael looked at his script. "Narciso, it is foolish for a man to appear here and there with a few fugitive verses. I want first to publish something definitive, a volume through which the public can get the perspective of my talent, if I have any."

"When will you have a volume ready?"

"If I could fight in a *corrida* every day, Narciso, very soon."

At this point the old peon woman came forward with little cups of black coffee. She sneezed as she came, but quickly repeated the formula, "Jesus, José, and Maria," to exorcise any evil the sneeze may have caused.

Angelito and his guests tossed down their black

nectar and then started out to Señor Montauban's motor which waited in the *calle*. The three men were in a hurry to catch the train to Valencia, so they stood in the doorway and made hissing sounds, "Psst! Psst! Psst!" up and down the *calle* in all directions, signaling for a boy to come and carry their trappings from the house to the motor. As they grew more impatient, their hissing became more intense. It looked as if they certainly must miss the train, when a boy came running out of a charcoal shop some three doors below. He came, carried out the equipment of the *toreros*, and deposited it in the car. The three men tumbled in hastily, flung the urchin a coin, and motored off.

By this time the mist had cleared away and the friends drove rapidly down Traposo *calle*, turned eastward, followed the electric track for some two miles, and found themselves at the station. This was two small houses set in a grove of magnificent trees and an unsheltered platform lying along a narrow-gage track. A blue-capped porter seized on the baggage of the travelers, inquired their destination, then hurried off, bought the tickets and checked their bags, so that all the *caballeroes* did was simply to sit in their motor and settle with the porter when he returned.

A number of passengers were waiting for the train
so the porters were kept very busy. At last came a
tootling down the track and a diminutive locomo-
tive with a string of four small cars rattled up to
the platform. Angelito and Rafael made their
adieus to Señor Montauban and got aboard the train.
The little coach they entered was just wide enough
for a double seat on one side and a single seat on
the other. The poet and the bullfighter got a double
seat together, and, after a brief bell-ringing, the
little train panted up into the mountains.

Angelito leaned back in his seat and looked out
of the window with a sense of pleasure at the changing view. For a little way they ran through a valley
with palms and tropical trees; then as they ascended
this gave way to stunted trees with great expanses
of yellow and green grass. The track wound tor-
tuously in and out among the mountain spurs.
Often the bullfighter could see the little engine
ahead. It always reminded him of some little dwarf
humped over, with legs flying and dashing along at
a great rate.

The track continually passed through small tun-
nels. Angelito could see these little holes lying far
ahead punched in the buttresses of the mountain.

It seemed extraordinary to think that his train could ever get through such tiny openings.

These little punctures accented the Cyclopean reach and swing of the Andes. Valleys dropped away from them to dizzy depths. Once Angelito saw a *saumari* sailing far below him, but evidently at a great height. Now and then the little train rattled across a bridge over some rocky gorge with a river boiling whitely far beneath. Noise of the waters reached him as a kind of whiffing at his ears and was gone.

Occasionally the train would stop at wayside stations, mere collections of *adobe* houses which looked as if they might have sprung up out of the earth of the mountains. Fruit venders offered their wares through the car windows. It was Angelito's impulse to buy some mamones, as he liked to ride in a train, watch the scenery unfold and break the little green globes of syrup in his mouth, but this time he did not purchase any on account of Rafael. He had observed that *caballeroes* did not eat on the train except at meal time.

At every station more peons crowded into the coaches armed with baskets and bottles, bent on making a fiesta and seeing the bullfight at Valencia.

The seats of the train were swiftly occupied and then the aisles became crowded. The peons talked noisily with each other. Some peered through the car windows and laughed excitedly at the speed the train was making. They ate their oranges, figs, bananas, and casabas, moved by the childlike impulse to make a holiday by eating endlessly.

Angelito watched their gustation with a faint envy. He saw them throw their peels and bottles out of the windows. And after all he could not see why men of Rafael's and Montauban's class did not please themselves in so simple a manner when they were on trains. The time had to be spent somehow. To gaze out of the car window and to taste mamone syrup, that was something. A girl and her father, both of the better class, sat just ahead of him. Something about the turn of the girl's cheek vaguely resembled Socorro Jiminez and reminded him of his adventure at the Jiminez villa. Then he recalled what Montauban had said about aspiring to be Rafael's brother-in-law. The idea struck Angelito somehow as incongruous; such a girl as Socorro Jiminez being married to such a smallish, rather dried-up fellow as the editor of *"Sol y Sombra."* He turned impulsively to his seat mate.

"Rafael," he asked, "is Señor Montauban your sister's fiancé?"

Rafael who was nearest the window was gazing with a far-away look at the unrolling panorama of the Andes. He withdrew his eyes and looked absently at the *torero*.

"Señor Montauban—pardon me, Angelito, what did you ask?"

"Is Señor Montauban your sister's fiancé?"

Rafael shrugged indifferently, "*Cá*! It may be, I don't know." He sat musing for several moments apparently thinking over the question and finally said: "Marriage is like this railroad track, a very trivial thing among mountains. I really doubt if one could magnify it sufficiently to be considered in a place like this. A man would be a fool to set a love tale among mountains. Perhaps Romeo and Juliet . . . or the Sapphic Odes . . ." He paused and seemed to decide against something for he shook his head, "No, quite impossible."

By this time Angelito was growing accustomed to gathering only a vague idea of what Rafael meant, and often none at all. He resumed his thoughts of the Señorita Jiminez and Señor Montauban while his eyes followed the hulls and rinds and bottles which the peons threw out of the windows.

Chapter 3

THE bull ring at Valencia is a big circular affair enclosed by a brick wall some ten feet high with the grandstand, or *"sombra"* section of the seats encircling its northern half. Entrance is obtained by two gates on the north side, and over these gates is painted the legend of all bull rings, *"Sol y Sombra."*

Bearing down on the *circo* from all quarters came cabs, motors, and pedestrians, while a great crowd of idlers were standing in the hot sunshine in the plaza, and would remain there throughout the *corrida,* sensing the progress of the fight by the roaring of the spectators.

As Rafael and Angelito drove up in a cab the legend above the entrance caught the poet's attention and he repeated the phrase aloud, "Sunshine and Shadow—I wonder which it will bring to me to-day, Angelito?"

At that moment Angelito was telling the driver to drive around to the south side of the ring.

"Aren't we going to the entrance?" asked the poet quickly.

"No, to the bull's entrance behind the ring."

"Ciertamente, I knew that."

The poet's eyes moved excitedly over the plaza, the gathering crowd, the blank brick walls as they drove around.

The bull's entrance on the southern side of the *circo* was a rough door set in the wall, and beside it stood a ramshackle old ambulance with two poor horses hitched to it. The intense heat reflected from the southern wall of the *circo* rose about the fighters as they got out of their cab. Angelito knocked at the bull's gate. It opened quickly and a tall limber-looking boy in a red shirt and blue trousers made him a bobbing bow.

"You beat us here, José," said the *torero* kindly.

"Sí, Señor," hissed José, grinning with pleasure at being addressed by the *diestro.* "Me and Jesus jumped off the train as soon as it stopped and ran here as fast as we could so we wouldn't be late."

Angelito smiled as he recalled the time when, as a *monosabio,* he ran to the *circo* as fast as he could, impelled by a terrible fear that he might be late.

A moment afterward the boy had the bullfighters' equipment out of the cab and the three entered the bull's gate together.

The fighters entered a little space fenced off from the arena by a high board wall.

On the east side of this small enclosure a shed had been erected to make a rough dressing room. Here half a dozen men and boys were dressing. The boys were putting on the red and blue uniforms of the *monosabios;* the men the bright colored trunks and tight jackets of *banderilleros.* Just beyond the eastern partition of the dressing room Angelito could hear the bulls moving in their stalls, and smell the ammoniacal scent of the animals mingled with the odor of decaying blood.

A priest in his cassock stood in the dressing room talking to the group. He had in his hands the crucifix and holy oil ready, in case of necessity, to administer extreme unction to the players.

When Angelito and Rafael entered, the priest came over to the *toreros* at once. He knew Angelito from former fights and offered his hand. The bullfighter bent and kissed it.

"How well you are looking, Angelito," he complimented. *"Cá!* A man can keep well in Caracas, up in the mountains, but here in Valencia, it is so hot . . ." He made a gesture expressive of the heat. *"Pues,* we have a great crowd to-day, the cathedral was jammed and a little army came to confession." He turned toward Rafael, "Whom have we here?"

"A *torero* who fights unknown, *padre*."

"*Caramba,* an unknown sword; that is romantic! I shall expect thrilling deeds from you, Señor, but— take care of yourself." He patted Rafael on the arm in paternal fashion.

At that moment out in the *circo* the municipal band began playing a waltz. The swing of the music went through Angelito. The *torero* always counted the music as the real beginning of a bull-fight. After that it climbed by ascending thrills to the death of the bull. He hoped the bulls would be steady animals for Rafael's sake. He had a feeling that he was Rafael's host and that he was personally responsible for his safety.

The two fighters began getting out of their citizen's clothes into their fighting regalia. Two *monosabios* acted as valets, laying out their trunks and jackets and stockings, capes, cloaks, sashes, and bandages.

Angelito's costume was green with silver beading. Rafael's was purple velvet with gold embroidery, and was the richer of the two. The *banderilleros* who were in the dressing room with the *diestros* wore travesties of this rich apparel. Their trunks and jackets were of bright cotton cloth ornamented with steel buttons. Angelito was rather ashamed of these men who were to be Rafael's fighting companions.

The last thing Angelito did was to arrange his pig-tail, brushing it upward and fitting over it his *mona*, a little black cap not as large as his fist. This *mona* and pigtail were the ancient badges of the bull-fighter's profession; they might possibly protect a man from being stunned and killed in case of a sudden fall.

A sour-faced man with a drooping mustache sud-denly appeared half-way down a ladder at the side of the shed. He waved an impatient arm at the fighters.

"*Pronto! Prisa!*" he urged. "The *circo* is full. The crowd is getting restless!" This apparently was addressed to the *banderilleros* for he spoke civilly enough to Angelito. "Are you nearly ready for the procession, Señor Angelito?"

"When the *padre* is ready," said the bullfighter.

At this the cleric stepped forward and the group of fighters turned to a crucifix hung on the east wall of the dressing room. This wall creaked oc-casionally from the movement of the bulls on the other side.

The priest placed his palms together and began a prayer for the safety of the fighters. He looked steadfastly at the crucifix and his Spanish was sonorous and fervent.

Angelito knelt stiffly on account of his tight knee buckles. He spread his arms to the figure and the cadaverous color of the body with its gouts of dull red paint reminded him of a victim of a bullfight. The stigma in the side might very well have been the thrust of a horn. The image moved a little now and then under the pressure of the animals on the other side of the wall.

The man clinging to the ladder did not pray because he was not going to fight. He was the promoter of the *corrida*. The moment the *padre* ceased praying he called briskly, "All right now; form line," and scrambled back up on the roof of the shed where he could overlook the arena.

As the brilliantly colored troupe stood silent in the stinking enclosure, Angelito glanced around to see how Rafael was accepting such poor surroundings. The poet was staring through the gate. *"Dios,"* thought Angelito, "I was stupid to bring such a man to this provincial *circo*. I should have dissuaded him."

The black mustached man on the roof, after scanning the formation in the little yard, waved a hand toward the arena. The band abruptly stopped the waltz and broke into a military march. Angelito straightened himself. The gates of the arena opened. On his eyes flared the wide yellow of the sand, the color of the sunshades and women's gala dresses gilding the great horseshoe of seats in the intense sunlight. The *torero* moved forward, and, keeping step to the music, marched at the head of the troupe into the hard sunlight of the amphitheater.

A burst of shouting came to Angelito like a shaking of the air. They were uproarious, these unaccustomed Valencians. He heard his own name shouted over and over in a confusion of music and *"Ole's!"* Not often did the premier *diestro* of Caracas come to Valencia.

He was glad that Rafael should hear this ovation. He was somebody even if not an *hidalgo* (son of somebody). The youth, too, could hardly avoid mentioning this uproar to his sister.

At the south of the ring the promoter of the fight still stood on top of the dressing room. He was waiting to lift a door in the southern wall of the arena to turn a bull into the ring. He gave a signal, the band ceased playing. Came that moment of suspense immediately before the drama of the bullfight.

From the northern rim of the arena a herald blew

a blast on his trumpet. The distant promoter pulled on an invisible rope and directly under him a black hole appeared in the yellow wall. Every eye in the amphitheater was fixed on this black target.

Angelito watched it and in his heart he hoped it would be some worthy bull, a noble bull. The head and horns of a big animal appeared in the dazzling sunshine. The man on the wall hurled two crimson rosettes downward and their iron barbs stuck deep in the bull's shoulders. Instantly the animal came snorting and plunging into the arena.

But a single glance told Angelito the bull was a failure. Instead of instantly singling out some enemy, the bull flung its head about and tried to rake the rosettes out of its shoulders. When a *monosabio* came near it, the animal would snort, shake its head, or make a half-hearted charge. It was a disgraceful bull.

Disgust went over Angelito. He knew no mortal man can tell whether or not a bull will fight, but nevertheless a tame bull just when he was keyed up to fight always tortured him.

One of the *banderilleros* did succeed in provoking the animal to charge him. He stamped his feet and waggled two red *banderillas* at the creature. At last the bull rushed. The man stood with his short red spears lifted as high as he could hold them, then he leaned over the horns of the charging bull, stuck the *banderillas* in the crest of the big shoulder immediately behind the rosettes, swung his body out of the way, and the bull charged past with two new torments in its shoulders.

But that was the last play they succeeded in getting out of the bull. After that it ran away from the men like a stray cow. After three or four minutes of aimless driving around the arena, the spectators began hissing and cat-calling. The promoter opened the door to the bull pen again and the *monosabios* drove the bull ignominiously through it. As it leaped through the gate it raked off one of the rosettes, and it lay, a little red mark in the glare of yellow sand.

Angelito was chagrined at this stupid *corrida*. That he had brought Rafael along somehow made it worse. He feared this poor exhibition would be retailed to Socorro Jiminez. He looked appealingly at Rafael amid the hisses and cat-calls. *"Demonio!* These provincials! No *circo,* no dressing room, no attendants, and no bulls! I'll never take another such engagement as long as I live!"

"Cá! The next bull may be better," suggested Rafael.

But the next bull was little better. When the promoter flung the rosettes into its shoulders it plunged into the arena in a rage and chased its bright-colored enemies behind the barriers, but its first rush did not last long. After the *banderilleros* had pinned a pair of darts in its shoulders, the bull grew wary. When it came time for the dart throwers to quit their play and for Angelito to bring about the animal's death, the *torero* had difficulty in luring the bull to attack at all. The big creature stood in the center of the arena with two yellow *banderillas* dangling from its streaked shoulders.

Angelito approached it, swung his red cape at it. The big brute simply pawed the ground and shook its horns. The *torero* advanced within three steps of the creature, swung his cloak almost against its nose. The bull lowered its head and charged. Its bulk passed under the red cape. Its high hump tossed up the *torero's* arms; its barrel barely grazed Angelito's stomach and legs. The smell of the hot animal enveloped him and he lifted a hand to wipe from his face a thread from its slavering muzzle.

Came a rattle of applause at this first interesting play; but the bull's fire was spent. Instead of charging again it moved away from the swordsman. Angelito, filled with shame and anger, followed it. He felt more like a neatherd than a *torero*. He shook his head, whipped his rapier in disgust so that all the spectators might see that he was disgusted. At last after Angelito had followed and stamped in an absurd fashion, the bull turned and faced him. The *torero* knew this would be the bull's last charge. He lifted the hilt of his rapier level with his eyes and sighted along the steel at the little spot right on top of the bull's shoulders through which he could strike the heart. Finally the animal charged. Angelito leaned toward the advancing bulk. He saw the tip of his rapier disappear between the shoulders. He thrust fiercely downward to sheathe his weapon in the huge animal. But the half-breed bull could not endure the steel. It swerved, jerked the rapier from Angelito's hands, and bolted with the weapon about half buried between its shoulders. At this mishap all the *banderilleros* ran out, trying to head off the bull. As the frightened animal ran past them they swung their red capes at the sword, trying to wrap them around the hilt and draw it out. The bull, quite beside itself with terror and pain leaped over the barrier into the inner runway. *Banderilleros* and *monosabios* opened a gate in the barrier and tried to drive the animal out. But blood began flowing from the brute's nostrils, presently it knelt in this narrow space, its hind parts tumbled against the fence. One of the *banderilleros* drew out the sword and brought it back to Angelito, wiping it on his cape as he came. A *monosabio* killed the bull and the old mules came jingling in, and dragged the dead animal out of the runway, across the arena and out of the bull's gate.

As the bull went out the herald blew a triumphant blast on his bugle and a moment later the band broke into a gay air. But this triumph was pure routine and without heart. There were cat-calls and hissings. A scattering of men arose in the boxes and began making their way toward the entrance. Others shouted *"Viejo toro!"* (old bull). "Give us our money back!" "This is no bull fight, it is a slaughter house!" "A lifeless old hide!" "We won't pay money to see beef killed!"

The *monosabios* pushed out barrows of sand to cover up a few red stains in the arena and shovel up some of the droppings of the tortured bull. But the red-shirted youngsters worked with embarrassment under the shadow of public disapproval. Angelito occasionally shook his head and whipped his sword to express his disgust. He was afraid the newspaper would advertise his fiasco. It might even prevent him from entering the big Spanish *corrida* which was approaching. *"Demonio,"* he growled to Rafael, "why did we ever come to Valencia!"

The promoter on the south side of the arena climbed down from the roof of the dressing room shed and later Angelito saw him coming up the passageway between the barriers and the seats. The grandstand likewise saw the approach of the promoter and a scattered cry of *"Fuego! Fuego!"* ran over the crowd.

The promoter hurried up to Angelito. "Señor," he cried among the noises of the spectators, "we must do something to hold the people. *Caramba!* Look how they are going away, and no doubt demanding their money back at the gate."

Angelito made a sharp gesture, *"Demonio,* I did not select these cowardly bulls!"

"Will you complain if I hearten them the best I can?"

The *torero,* knowing what the promoter was hinting at, said, "But think of my standing as a fighter!"

"Sangre de Cristo!" cried the fellow in anguish. "Shall I lose all my gate money on account of your standing as a fighter! Will you disappoint the

crowd in a great religious fiesta on account of your standing as a fighter!"

More cries of *"Fuego! Fuego!"* came from the seats and the promoter made a despairing gesture.

Rafael shrugged. *"Cá!* Let him go ahead. In the provinces one must be a provincial!"

Angelito stood out a little longer, saying it was cruel, *"inordinato,"* but Rafael's desertion decided the matter. The impresario made a gesture of agreement, and turned back toward the bull pen again. *"Caramba,* what a fight!" snapped Angelito.

But the spectators were suddenly on the *qui vive.* Came a clatter of applause, while men who were going out turned back to their seats. More cries of *"Fuego!"* Women waved their sunshades.

The promoter reappeared on the shed. The crowd roared, because his distant figure held two flaming torches in its hands. In the midst of the uproar came the buoyant fanfare of the herald. At these penetrating notes complete silence fell over the arena.

The promoter opened the door of the bull pen. An instant later the head of a black bull appeared in the opening. The promoter lifted his fiery torches and hurled them down into the shoulders of the brute.

An instant whirl of action. The bull with flames leaping from his back charged in a fury of pain at the bright colored gadflies that danced before him. The spectators, gathered to celebrate the holy fiesta, shrieked, howled, flung up hats, sunshades, and stamped with ecstasy.

The bull shot like a huge black bolt at everything that moved. *Banderilleros* dashed into the barriers while their fellows drew the endless charge.

A man in yellow came out with yellow *banderillas*. The bull hurtled at him. The player lifted his darts, leaned over, but his haste in striking threw him out of balance and he stuck the *banderillas* awkwardly, one down on the bull's shoulder, the other too far up his neck. A disgraceful play; they should have been neatly paired just behind the rosettes.

However the spectators at the fiesta roared on joyously, not regarding this point of art and symmetry, "Fire! Fire!" They were happy. But the ragged *banderillas* and the applause irritated Angelito. *"Caramba!* These Valencianoes are animals!" he thought. "They applaud stupidities!" Then he saw that Rafael was selecting a rapier from four or five offered him by a *monosabio*.

Angelito looked at his friend in alarm. "Rafael," he called above the applause, "I will do this. That bull is crazed. It is no ordinary risk—your sister . . ."

The poet whipped out a sword. "God's lightning! Don't I escape my mother and sister in Valencia?" He sighted down the thin ribbon of the blade which looked like watered silk.

"But, Rafael," warned the bullfighter, "you are going in too early, let the *banderilleros* wear him down a bit!"

For answer the youth picked up his red cape, whipped his rapier under it so as to hold out the crimson silk on the steel.

Angelito stepped forward and touched his arm, "*Mi amigo*, I tell you it is dangerous now, very dangerous; I wouldn't do it myself!"

But the spectators saw the poet advancing with sword and cape into the yellow ring and new gusts of applause swept over them. "*Magnifico! A guapo! Invicto!*"

Angelito stood by the barrier watching the slender figure in purple and gold walk out on the sand with the light step of a trained fighter. He thought of Socorro again, and what the girl would do if anything should happen to Rafael.

The *banderilleros* were now playing the bull toward the center of the ring. When they had lured him in front of Rafael, the whole troupe dashed for the barriers. The sudden shift from these flying colored figures to this single purple fighter standing quietly in the sunshine brought even the tortured bull to a standstill.

About the young aristocrat hung a natural grace which none of the other performers even approached. A wave of the crimson silk cape and the black monster flashed at the youth. The bull whipped up the silk with its bulk; it wheeled and came again. With a curving gesture of his cape, Rafael seemed to swing the great black bulk to the other side. The flaming animal passed under his outstretched arms, and the youth drew the bull around once again.

The poet's finesse looked as simple and rhythmic as dancing. The spectators watched this play of flame, color, and danger in the brilliant sunshine in absolute silence. Angelito stared at it as if hypnotized. What a *diestro* the youth was! What a marvel!

In Angelito's thoughts, Rafael's skill wound itself about his sister Socorro. *Dios in cielo!* What a *señorita* she must be! What a brother, what a sister!

Something struck Angelito on the back of his

hand. He looked down. A piece of jewelry lay on the sand. A sudden uproar broke from the amphitheater; silver, coins, fans, kerchiefs fell into the bull ring.

As Angelito looked around at this spontaneous applause, a kind of gasp went over the crowd. The *torero* knew that gasp. He whirled. The next moment he seized a rapier and dashed across the sand toward the fight. As the bull charged, flame and smoke from the torches had whipped the poet in the eyes.

Angelito saw the bull lunging straight at the youth. He saw Rafael give back blinking, lift his rapier and try to defend himself. The point struck a bone as the brute lunged. The blade doubled and snapped. The next moment the huge head was under the fighter. As the bull tossed, the slender figure was flung high over the black head. The body fell on the black hind quarters, then was thrown to the sand. The bull whirled to impale the purple figure when Angelito flung himself on the monster blanketing the head in his red cape. An instant later the *torero* himself was rushed backward, caught between the bull's horns.

Amphitheater, *banderilleros*, the sand beneath him, became a blur of flying color to the *torero*. All

Angelito saw distinctly was the red cape over the head and the flying black shoulders with the sputtering rosettes of flame. But before the bull could toss him, the *torero* had shortened his rapier and stabbed furiously at the great head under the red cloth. His long training in the Matadero guided his steel. It struck home in the little unprotected spot over the spinal cord. Next moment the bull collapsed. The *torero* went tumbling backwards along the sand, but he rolled like a gymnast, came up on his feet with a perfect sense of direction and without a pause went running to Rafael.

The *banderilleros* were picking the youth up. The poet's beautiful face was chalky. His great black eyes turned on Angelito. With a terrible pang, the bullfighter thought of Socorro Jiminez.

"O Wounds of Christ!" gasped the *torero*, putting his arms about Rafael to help carry him. "Beloved comrade, are you deeply gored?"

The figure in the arms of the men shrugged faintly, attempted to smile, then closed its eyes against the glare of the sun.

The amphitheater was roaring with ecstasy; it was a-flutter with rainbows. In the midst of this storm of delight the herald blew a shrill note of triumph. The door of the bull pen opened; the old

mules trotted out and dragged the dead bull out of
the ring. Rafael's crimson cape was left alone in the
yellow arena.

That afternoon as the train from Valencia climbed
back across the Andes, Angelito sat in the baggage
car beside the litter on which Rafael lay. The
espada's seat was a bale of cloth from one of Valencia's cloth mills. Angelito sat humped over, chin
in hands, with a dozen miserable thoughts gnawing
at his brain. He felt himself culpable for agreeing
to fight a bull tortured by flambeaux. He thought
of the grief so soon in store for Socorro Jiminez and
her mother. Occasionally there flickered through
his mind what the papers would say about his fight
at Valencia. They might very well discredit him
and lose for him all part in the great Spanish *corrida* which was approaching. Then his thoughts
would return to Socorro Jiminez. What would the
girl think of him?

The unhappy fellow fished with his forefinger under his collar and drew up his rosary. He began
passing the beads through his fingers, his lips moving to the appropriate prayers; but his thoughts
clung about the wounded poet, the sister, the
wretchedness he was bringing her, the newspapers,

the coming Spanish *corrida* from which he might be
barred, the sister again.

It seemed to Angelito that Socorro Jiminez had
been for him a distant possibility, but now he could
hardly hope to gain her glance again. . . .

A white sheet was drawn over the poet up to his
chin. His pale carved face shook to the tremors
of the train. A terrifying thought struck Angelito
that the poet was dead, but at that moment the black
eyes opened and looked at the bullfighter. Angelito
leaned over and put his ear close to Rafael's lips.

"Do you want something, Rafael?"

"You—mustn't—tell—Socorro."

"No, I won't." Then Angelito happened to think
that this was absurd. "How can I help it, Rafael?"

"Take—me—to—your—*casa*."

"I could do that." The fighter was rather surprised at the suggestion. "They will be expecting
you to return."

"Tell her—I have gone—to the Tuy—family
estate on the Tuy."

Angelito nodded. "Yes, I'll do that, Rafael."

The poet lay without speaking, pressing his lips
together in his stresses of pain. Angelito leaned
over him, yearning to do something to ease the jolting of the train. He slipped his palms under the

wounded man's dark rumpled hair and held the weight of his head. Thus supported the sufferer looked weakly through the door of the baggage car.

"Sunset," he whispered, "the end of the day."

The bullfighter followed the stricken man's gaze. Through the rectangle of the door he saw the red upheaved clouds of an Andean sunset rising up from the abysses below. Some dark and monstrous cauldron was boiling red and purple vapors against a sky of tingling blues and greens.

The bullfighter recalled the poem Rafael had read that morning and he knew that his friend was thinking of his verses now.

Such a feeling of pathos seized Angelito that tears welled from his eyes and dropped between his outstretched arms. He felt sure that his friend would die. It seemed because Rafael had written the poem this evil had come upon him.

The thought of Socorro Jiminez mingled with this tragedy. All the imagery and fineness of the poet, his grace and daring in the *corrida,* his silent endurance of the jolting of the train, and now his weak sad gazing at the sunset, all these endearing finenesses somehow inhered also in Socorro Jiminez. She, too, was fine, brave, patrician, sensitive, and patient, somehow in a more exquisite way than

Rafael himself. At moments it seemed to Angelito that through her brother he was in some way ministering to the girl herself, and for her his tears were falling.

Chapter 4

WITH the installation of Rafael as a patient in the front room of the blue *casa* on Traposo *calle*, medicos and sisters of charity became familiars of the house. The front room with its frieze of rose vases, crossed rapiers, and religious lithographs now reeked of disinfectants and at Rafael's bedside arose the melancholy scaffolding of a Murphy's Drip, with its elevated tank and its tubes which ran down into the poet's wounds and out again into a slop jar. The faint tap, tap, tap of the solution might have been the poet's life dripping away.

With such a terrible example of the injuries which might be received from a bullfight constantly before her eyes, the old peon woman, Angelito's mother, went about her work mumbling continual prayers for the safety of her son. On this particular morning she was in her own room, a little den far to the rear of the *patio* which had been made for servants and which she chose instinctively for her room, when her son had moved her out of the squalor of the Matadero district to this *casa*.

To give point to her reverie she was still stitching the rents in Rafael's fighting trunks where the bull's horns had penetrated. She had washed the blood from the fabric, but the torn places still frightened her and she was hardly able to control her stitches.

"Oh, madre in cielo!" she prayed, blinking her eyes as she bent over the work. "My poor Pancho, some day, some day . . . " She broke off, shaking her old head fearfully, when the door opened without any formality, and Angelito put in his head.

"Have you got it fixed, *madre?*" he asked.

"In a moment, *hijo* (son). Won't you come in?"

The bullfighter hesitated, glanced up the *patio* to see if any one were in sight, then stepped inside and closed the door behind him. He looked about in distaste. *"Caramba,* what a room. As much like our old hovel in the Matadero as two peas."

"This is much drier, *hijo.*"

"And your lottery tickets and your peppers and your yammi roots. He stood looking about the dirt floor in the depth of disgust. His eyes paused on a kind of board stuck full of lottery tickets such as the street venders carry around on the streets of Caracas.

"*Madre,* how often have I asked you never again to sell a lottery ticket?"

The old creature looked stubbornly at the tickets.

"It makes money, Pancho."

"Three thousand devils!" he stormed. "We have enough money! Look at this *casa,* fifteen or twenty rooms. *Valgame Dios,* I don't know how many rooms and you pick the worst one. I have bought you dresses and you wear that old skirt; I buy shoes and you wear *alpargatas,* and now you sell lottery tickets for more money!"

The old peon woman stitched silently on the torn velvet trunks, then she asked doggedly, "Why don't you give up fighting bulls, Pancho?"

The man stared at her. "*Caramba,* I have to have money to run all this."

"But why run it!" cried the peon woman. "You could sell this *casa* and live forever in safety. You need never take another risk."

Angelito looked at his mother and drew down his lips, "How long do you think my friends would recognize me, *madre,* if I lived in such a hovel as you have in mind?"

"*Ay de mi,*" sighed the old peon, "if your friends really loved you, Pancho, they could not endure to see you risk your life in the *circo* every Sunday. That would break their hearts."

"*Madre*," exclaimed the fighter impatiently, "you do not understand. Aristocratic friends are not like peon friends. Peons fall in with each other anyway, rich or poor, clad or naked, full or hungry they are always the same. But friendship among aristocrats is more like a game. One must be prepared to play, or *Cá!*, one can't play! Aristocrats have standards, something to live up to, a fine *casa*, honor, bravery, money. If you fail to have these out you go among the peons. That is fair. Friendship among the aristocrats is a game like a bullfight."

"*Valgame Dios*," cried the old peon woman, throwing up her hands, "then is not a peon friend a thousand times better and more faithful than a *caballero* friend?"

"Not at all. The peon is at the bottom and can lose nothing. Since he has no rank he requires none. Look at me. I am no longer a peon. I have carved a place for myself among the *caballeros* with my rapier. I hold my place with my rapier. They are my dear friends, naturally, as long as I hold my place. You see the *caballeros* are really more faithful than the peons, they are faithful to their standards: honor, bravery, power . . ."

"What you call faithfulness to standards," cried the old woman, "is just selfishness. For you to wear fine clothes and spend money on them pleases them, and they won't put up with you unless you do."

"*Seguro,* it is as I say, they live to standards, principles. The Son of the Virgin taught us that, *madrecita,* to live for principles." Angelito crossed himself.

"*Huy,* a fine son you are to say it is religion to desert your friends when they meet misfortune! That is what comes of talking to aristocrats and learning their wickedness!" She tossed the mended trunks point-blank at her son. "There, why were you in such a hurry to get them?"

"I want to return them."

"He can't use them, never again, poor *joven.*"

"I want to carry them to his villa and tell he has gone to the Tuy."

The old woman looked at the fighter sharply. "*Cá!* You are going to carry them to the villa?"

"Yes," nodded Angelito a little uncomfortably.

The old lottery ticket vender grimaced. "*Caramba,* do you imagine she would look twice at you if it wasn't for your money and your *casa.* What a fool you are, Pancho! You say yourself the aristocrats care for nothing except what you can give them, and then you jump about, 'Hurry, *madre!* Get the trunks fixed, *madre!*' and off you rush to the villa to speak to this fortune hunter!"

Angelito's swarthy skin darkened. "No, I am not a fool, *madre*. When you are an aristocrat you try to get what you want. It is a game. If she did not get money and a villa she would lose her place; if I did not marry some soft pale girl in silk, I would lose my place. I say it is a game, *madre*, like bullfighting. There is a great deal more to bullfighting than just the money you get out of it. And there is a great deal more to marrying an aristocrat than just the name and power she brings you. An aristocrat is a fine thing in itself and that's why name and power go with it."

The old woman got up with furious tears in her eyes. *"Demonio!* I'm sorry I ever fixed the dirty things for you!"

The *torero* turned out of the room into the *patio*. *"Diabolo,* I don't see why I ever stop to talk to you!"

Angelito made a bundle of the clothes and started out of the *casa* wondering whether or not he ought to withhold the knowledge of Rafael's injuries from the Jiminez family. On his way out he stopped at the front room to see the poet. A sister of mercy at the bedside beckoned him not to enter, then arose and came to the door herself.

"Señor Jiminez had a very bad night," she whispered, glancing about at her patient. "He was delirious and kept calling for pencil and paper."

"Pobrecito!" said the *torero*. "He wanted to write something."

"Sí, Señor; then he began repeating some poetry and wanted me to take his dictation. Finally I gave him some powders just before daylight. He is still asleep." She looked around at her patient.

"Poetry," mused the bullfighter, looking at Rafael's shadowy face among the pillows. He could not understand how the setting of words in line could so burn a man up with desire.

"Is he going to get well?" he whispered to the sister.

"He is young, Señor, and God is very merciful to the young." She crossed herself with a hand roughened from service.

"I am going to his house," explained Angelito. "He asked me not to tell his mother and sister."

"Is his mother an invalid?" asked the nurse.

"I—don't know," hesitated Angelito, a little dubious about telling the sister a falsehood. The nun returned to her seat. Angelito picked up his bundle and moved slowly out of the *casa*. In the *calle* he hailed a passing cab and set out for Paraiso.

As Angelito rode southward he knew that the Señora and the Señorita Jiminez would immediately find the rents in the clothing and he began inventing a story to answer the questions which they would most certainly ask. He decided to say a *novillo* had flung him on the fence and had torn his clothing. Then he would add, as if from a sudden memory: "Oh, yes, and I forgot to tell you that Rafael has gone down to the Jiminez estate on the Tuy. He said he would be there for a few days." The bull-fighter thought this plan would give Rafael's absence an inconsequential air. "Oh, yes, I forgot to tell you, etc., etc." And all the while he would be handing in the torn garments and Rafael would be lying pale and shadowy in the front room with the ghastly tubes running into him and out of him. "Down on the Tuy for a few days, looking after the Jiminez estate . . ."

By the time he had the details of this narrative worked out the driver was halting beside the high stone pillars and tall iron fence of the Jiminez villa. Angelito directed the cabman to follow with the bundle, opened the big gate, and set out down the path toward the house.

Once it struck Angelito as a queer thing that he never approached the Jiminez villa without busily planning what he meant to say; but this curious fact was swiftly forgotten as he ascended the steps, rang the bell, and once more nervously assembled his speech, "I am sorry, Señorita, that I tore Rafael's clothes, but a *novillo* tossed me . . . etc., etc."

In the midst of this rehearsal came a sound of quick footsteps in the hallway, and a moment later the inner door opened and not the maid but the Señora and the Señorita Jiminez appeared. Both women were greatly excited. "Where's Rafael!" cried the Señora and began undoing the bronze shutter, while the Señorita immediately added: "What's happened to him? He has been gone from home two nights! Do you know anything about this?" She rattled a newspaper at Angelito.

By this time the Señora had unfastened the grill and she and the Señorita rushed out on the fighter and surrounded him with a faint cool fragrance.

The *torero's* rehearsed phrases long since had flown.

"About what, Señorita?" he asked vacantly.

"This!" the Señorita shook the newspaper at him, unfolded it and pointed to the first page. She began reading the headlines in a shaken voice. "Son of

Illustrious Caraqueno Family Desperately Wounded in *Corrida* at Valencia. Nameless *Torero* Tossed by Bull after Series of Daring Passes. Barbarous Custom of Using Flambeaux on Bull Causes Disaster."

The girl suddenly seized Angelito's arm and shook it. There were tears in her eyes. "That's Rafael; there is not another *joven* in all Caracas so mad as to do such a thing!" She shook Angelito's arm again. "Where is he? What have you done with him?"

"God's mercy!" cried Angelito entirely nonplussed by this attack. "I know nothing about him!"

"Weren't you in Valencia with him?"

"*Caramba!* No, Señorita!"

"You are the man who carried him his clothes and rapier!"

"No, no, I borrowed them for myself!"

"Oh, Holy Virgin!" cried the Señora despairingly. "Is there no way to get the truth out of a peon!"

"But, Señora, I say I fought at a fight of young bulls."

"You carried those clothes straight to Rafael," sobbed the Señora, "and now my poor boy is dead! I know he's dead! He's dead!" The handsome woman fell to weeping miserably.

"No, *madre!*" cried the girl. "No, Rafael is wounded and he sent this *bribon* up here to say he is all right. I know that's what he has done, it's exactly what he would do!" Socorro's black eyes glistened with tears. She turned on Angelito and rather took his breath, "Now where is he?"

"Señorita!" cried Angelito entirely unable to shift his plans so suddenly, "Rafael has simply gone down to the Jiminez estate on the Tuy for a few days . . ."

Socorro gave a little cry, "Oh! Oh! That proves what I said is true!"

"*Caramba,* how?" cried the *torero.*

"You would never have known we had an estate on the Tuy if Rafael hadn't told you!"

"*Ciertamente* he told me!" cried Angelito excitedly. "He told me when I returned his clothes to tell you that."

"Did you go with him to the Tuy?"

"*Seguro,* no! I fought at a fight of young bulls."

"At Valencia?"

"No, near the Matadero. We hired a young bull."

"On the fiesta?"

"*Ciertamente,* Señorita."

"Then if Rafael was in Caracas on the fiesta why

didn't he come home that night; there is only one
train a day to the Tuy?"

The Señora controlled her sobs long enough to
plead in her deep tones, "Please, please, Señor, don't
tell us any more lies. Where is Rafael—is he
dead?"

"No!" cried Angelito distractedly. "He is not
dead. He is in the blue *casa* at the *eschino Miercoles
y Traposo.*"

At this the two women started impetuously for the
cab at the gate.

"Por l'amor de Dios!" cried the bullfighter hurrying after them. "Don't go rushing in like that,
you'll upset him. He's asleep!"

But the women went on flying down the path sobbing and praying under their breaths. Angelito followed and a moment later saw them get into his cab
and drive away through the sunshine.

Angelito tramped back to the Jiminez gate astonished and chagrined at the outcome of his performance. After the cab and the ladies were quite out
of sight he could still feel distinctly the place on his
arm where the Señorita Jiminez had caught him and
urged him to tell the truth. That to a *caballero!
Diantre,* she did not know, she could not see that

he was trying to protect her and her mother! He made violent gestures to these mental exclamations. *Diabolo,* the stupidity of women!

He let himself out of the gate and moved along the handsome boulevard thinking over an imaginary conversation with her. At first he railed at her, showed her her injustice, her ingratitude. It was a white lie he was telling her, one meant to bring her peace of mind. She had called him a liar when the holy saints knew that she was addressing a man whose whole heart was for her a well of truth.

"My feeling for you, Señorita," soliloquized Angelito, murmuring the words in the most appealing tones, "is as the hermit for the saint he adores. I have often thought of you as a kind of handmaid of heaven who is lowered in a glory to see me risk my life in the *circo,* and then you vanish away, your grace, your sweetness, your beauty, and I can bring you back only by risking my life again and again. And He Who Reads Men's Hearts knows that I would court danger and even death itself rather than never to see you again."

Angelito's inner voice was now trembling with tears and he was moved by his fancy to tell Socorro good-by, although there was no reason why he should not have pursued his meditation for the rest of the day had he so desired. Perhaps he was growing a little weary of her image and did not realize it. At any rate she was going, "Then *adios*, Señorita," he trembled; "you call me false; it is the falseness of a yearning heart that would give its hope of heaven to remove one shadow from your joy, one single thorn from . . ."

His reverie did not stop as a conversation might stop, it simply grew thinner, more tenuous, the trembling voice seemed to sink into some mental distance, still protesting, still worshiping, and was gone.

About the same time that his pleading vanished, somebody called Angelito's name. The bullfighter looked up and saw a small, very trig gentleman in a formal black coat and pearl gray trousers whisking a cane. It was Señor Montauban and this was rather surprising. The surprise was not that Señor Montauban should have been strolling on Paraiso, for his home was along here somewhere, but that in such a place he should have called Angelito's name.

"Out promenading, I see," smiled Señor Montauban, looking with a certain curiosity at the *torero*.

Angelito decided not to admit promenading too

far. "I thought I would stretch my legs as far as the Puente de Hierro; I'll catch a tram there."

The editor waited for Angelito to come up and then actually turned and fell in at his side.

"I hope," said Señor Montauban earnestly, "that you called by the Jiminez villa and told the ladies what you know about Rafael; they are quite disturbed over the poor boy."

"Yes, I did," nodded the *torero*, more and more amazed at his growing inclusion in Paraiso life.

"Did you really?" Montauban glanced up at the big fellow, then added, "That was very thoughtful."

"*Sí*," assured Angelito expanding, "I let them know Rafael was at my *casa* and immediately they rushed out, took my cab and drove up there. You should have met them."

While these words told a verbal truth, the manner in which Angelito said it conveyed an impression that the Jiminez family had received him in the most intimate way and had taken the cab of an old friend.

"*Caramba!*" ejaculated the editor, looking at him quite frankly now. "I knew you and Rafael knew each other, but—*Cá!* Paraiso is the boulevard where one must be acquainted, if one expects to know any one at all. Now you, Señor . . . " Narciso broke off, "Pardon me, Señor, but may I ask what is your real name? One can hardly address a friend of the Jiminez family by the name he uses in the *circo*."

The question caught Angelito unprepared. He was even uncertain whether or not it was asked in good faith. He tried to decide this point while he formed an answer and the dual operation confused him. It would never do to say his name was Pancho Pachecho—*Madre in cielo!* A peon named Pancho Pachecho promenading Paraiso with Narciso Montauban. Impossible! He moistened his lips. "My name really is—er—Angel," said the *torero*, "Gabrielo Angel, and I made it little Angel (Angelito) to be like the rest of the *toreros*."

"Juan Leon uses his own name," observed Montauban.

"Yes, I had thought about using mine. I don't like my placards somehow, Señor Montauban. The other day in Malestar's wineshop I was looking at my placards; I don't know, but somehow I don't like them."

Señor Montauban had a faintly dried-looking skin and now his smile made it look a trifle drier and crinklier. "I have never noticed, but you know there is one thing I cannot understand about men like you and Juan Leon; how you can fight bulls for money. Certainly I know the charm of a bullfight, the color, the light, the high zest of soul, but how any one can do it for money—so much zest for so much money!" The editor spread his hands. "It's rather grotesque."

Angelito had never faced such an attack as this in all his life. It was a most extraordinary viewpoint. *"Pues,"* he said thoughtfully, "you print articles in *'Sol y Sombra'* for money. Tito Monnico paints pictures for money."

" *'Sol y Sombra,' sí*. We old families must recoup our fortunes; if we do not . . ." Narciso made an expressive gesture, "we drown. We are lost in a tide of half-breed blood that is sweeping over Venezuela. You, who are trying to hold your head above water here in Paraiso know that as well as the rest of us."

Angelito nodded, not very clear on just which side of the fence the editor was placing him. Señor Montauban continued: *"Sí,* the old *conquistador* blood of Venezuela is being diluted, thinned, lost. *Mestizo,* upstarts, *griffes, zambos,* part Negro, part Carib, part Spanish, *Diabolo* knows what goes into them! What vessels to preserve the ancient Spanish ideals, the old Spanish manners, courtesy, art, magnificence, and power! Do you imagine such half-breeds can reproduce the Spanish soul? *Absurdo!*

"Look at Caracas; possibly there are ten pure-blooded Spanish families in the city! Ten left out of the hundreds of thousands Spanish cavaliers who conquered this rich country. Read the roll of *caballeros* who set this country free, once an honorable roll, Señor Angel, but boiled down to mongrels now!"

The editor shook his head. "What is left of us is vanishing. Any *mestizo* with a little money immediately reaches out for a *señorita,* and she is lost, her children are lost, the race is lost, for a race stands or falls through its women, Señor Angel."

A queer internal trembling set up in Angelito. The editor was a most surprising little man, he had the strangest ideas. Through his monologue, Angelito scented an attack on himself. Angelito knew that his father had in him merely a strain of Spanish and his mother none at all, but that was no reason why he, Angelito, should not be as good as anybody. If that was what Señor Montauban meant . . . still the editor seemed to be talking of other folk, the *mestizos,* the *griffes,* the *zambos* . . ." All An-

gelito could do was to move along by the editor's
side and nod occasionally.

They came to the Puente de Hierro (the bridge
of Iron) which was a long viaduct that spanned the
Guayra River in the south of Caracas. The viaduct
crossed the wide fertile valley of the river and spread
below it were great truck and banana groves. At
regular intervals along the sides of the viaduct arose
royal palms and their crests glittered high in the
sunshine.

At the Puente de Hierro the two men separated,
Angelito crossing it into the heart of the city. As
the bullfighter moved across the bridge he looked
down and saw some half-dozen peons at work in the
grove below. They moved in and out under the
great leaves of the banana plants, digging about their
roots, hacking off a dead leaf and dragging it out of
the way. Angelito knew they were toiling for a certain Señor Boncillo who owned the field and had a
box at the *circo*. A disturbing emotion rose up in
Angelito, vague and formless. He moved on again,
and toward the north he saw a thin yellow trail zig-
zagging up the enormous massif of the mountains.
The peons had made that, too.

Chapter 5

AMONG the bullfighters, *banderilleros,* and *aficionados* who foregathered in old Malestar's wineshop in Candelaria plaza, there circulated a daily grist of gossip as to what was happening at the blue *casa* on Traposo *calle.*

The bullfighters themselves could not decide whether the desirable or the undesirable had happened to Angelito. A lean-faced mulatto, whose greasy crinkly hair was drawn tightly back in a bullfighter's cue, leaned over the table, slid out a double nine domino and vented this philosophy.

"At any rate both the Señora and the Señorita Jiminez are all but living in the blue *casa* now nursing Rafael; every hour some great carriage stops in front of his house and 'tr-r-ring' goes his doorbell; in steps a banker maybe to inquire about Rafael; then 'tr-r-ring' and now it's an editor, 'tr-r-ring' next a *señorita,* all walking just so . . . " The mulatto straightened himself in his chair, composed his face to a preternatural gravity and imitated the callers entering the blue *casa.* The *aficionados* burst out laughing.

"Cá!" ejaculated an old man. "I don't know whether the aristocrats find any pleasure in life or not, always wearing clean clothes and collars and shoes and talking on dull subjects, but it isn't reasonable that they would do these unpleasant things day after day unless there was some good point to it. So if Angelito really has become an aristocrat, maybe his taste has changed. *Cá!* You can never tell about a man!"

A *banderillero* with his eyes in pouches from dissipation winked and observed that any man was likely to wear collars when a *señorita* was in his *casa,* and conversation with such a *bicho* was never dull.

"*Caramba,* yes," put in the mulatto with tight hair, "but she stays constantly at her brother's bedside. Yet the money Angelito throws away on that *chica!* Why only the other day a peon drove his donkey loaded with flowers down from the mountain past the blue *casa.* When this *señorita* saw the donkey through the window she cried out, 'How beautiful!' And this mad man, Angelito, who was at the door to ask about his friend, immediately exclaimed, 'It is yours, Señorita!'

"Both the *señorita* and her mother tried to stop him, but no, he ran out into the *calle* and bought all the flowers and hired the donkey to stand all day in his *patio*, loaded just as it was where the *señorita* could look out and see it. Just fancy a flower donkey standing among the pink columns of Angelito's *patio* for an ornament!"

The circle broke out laughing again. "Do they eat at his *casa?*" inquired some one.

"*Ola*, there's a point!" proceeded the humorous mulatto. "I met Doña Ana at the *mercadero* the other morning. She had her board of lottery tickets, for she never goes to market without taking her tickets and trying to sell enough to pay for her purchases. Well, she saw me and cried, 'Conchito! Conchito! Come here quickly!'

" 'What do you mean?' I asked.

" 'Conchito, the Jiminezes have settled on us like locusts. You will have to buy two tickets from me to-day. I must have this basket full.'

"*Naturalmente*, I bought two tickets, for when Doña Ana starts to sell you anything you have bought it already. She went on talking as I chose my numbers: 'That little baggage called Margherita Miraflores will eat with us. My poor demented son insisted and insisted. God's blood, all they want out of my poor Pancho is something to eat and flowers. It's a great pity there are any aristocrats in the whole world, Conchito.'

" 'That may be true, Doña Ana,' I said, 'but aristocrats threw to Angelito the pearl bangles in your ears.'

" '*Cá!*' She hunched up her shoulders. 'Perhaps they are that much service, but let them keep their distance. Aristocrats should know their places, Conchito, and not come forcing themselves where they are not wanted!' She was very angry and elbowed her way around among the stalls. I watched what she bought, *cassava* bread, yammi, plantains, rice, and chicken, a regular peon's mess to serve to her guests. And she bought loads of everything as the peons do when they make a feast."

Some of the gossips laughed at this, some sat silent. After a while a *banderillero* in a cheap coat asked, "Conchito, how is it possible to make a feast in any other way than to buy a great deal of everything?"

"*Caramba!* You can buy fine things, unusual things, something to astonish your guests."

"*Pues,* what unusual things?"

"*Cá!* Erculito, I can think of nothing unusual just at this moment; you are *loco* to expect it, but if a great army of aristocrats should march into my *casa*, I am sure they would have a fine tale to tell of Conchito's table, for instance, tea instead of coffee. Tea is a very rare, fine drink, Erculito. It tastes something like dishwater."

Old Malestar's wineshop might have been more loquacious and humorous had it known the inner workings of Angelito's feast and how remote was Angelito from his guests. How the bullfighter saw the Señorita Jiminez moving in and out of Rafael's sick room as inaccessible as a figure in a painting.

As nearly friendly as she ever became was a *"Buenos dias, Señor"* of mornings and a word or two about Rafael's condition when Angelito came to inquire each forenoon and evening. Once or twice as he stood talking to Rafael, Angelito noticed the Señorita looking intently at him. He wondered what she thought. He had not the remotest idea.

Such slight contacts, however, were sufficient to keep Socorro Jiminez perpetually in the bullfighter's mind. When he was away from her he spent much of his time fancying himself with her and talking to her. He conducted long monologues with her image, flattery in the hyperbolic strain of peons, out-bursts of tenderness and passion. And the upshot of it all was a feverish feeling in his head and the knowledge that presently Rafael would be taken back to Paraiso, and that this fair girl would go from his *casa* to return no more. After that all that he would ever see of her would be glimpses caught from the *circo*, a distant figure in the sunshine leaning over the balustrade watching him graze death for her amusement. For the first time in his life Angelito felt the irony of amusing people by risking destruction. It was an amazing thing that he should bring a keen pleasure to Socorro Jiminez and to ten thousand other *aficionados* by taking dangerous chances or by getting killed. It was a disquieting riddle, one that Angelito lacked the subtlety to read.

One morning Angelito took this conundrum to his little garden at the back of his *casa*. This little ground was only some forty feet square. It was surrounded by high brick walls and was overgrown with wild guava bushes and a spraddling tamarind tree in the corner. In the center was a small concrete basin of water and the only inhabitant of this garden was a white heron with clipped wings. This heron was always morose and when any stranger came into the garden it would elevate its delicate crest in anger and charge the intruder, threatening to stab with its long lanciform beak. However it never really struck any one. If a person stood his ground, the heron's crest would fall and it would hide away among the bushes. However if the intruder gave an inch, the bird would chase him out of the garden. Angelito was fond of tossing live fish into the basin and watching the snow-white bird spear them. On this particular morning he had two small fishes and as he went down into the garden he met Señorita Miraflores coming out rather hastily, and behind her came the heron with crest erect.

Angelito laughed outright and explained the fowl's cowardice. The *señorita* turned on the slender-legged bird and it darted away at once. Only by flinging a fish into the basin did Angelito persuade it to come out of the guavas.

Margherita became interested in the bird's expert fish spearing and was amused at her own flight from such a blusterer.

"I think a great many formidable looking birds, and persons, too, might be vanquished, Señor Angelito, by the display of a very little courage."

The Señorita Miraflores was short, very pretty, and always appeared gay and friendly. Her expression was so quizzical that the bullfighter looked at her quickly.

"For instance who, Señorita?"

"*Caramba,* your heron for one!" She broke into very pretty soft laughter.

The extremely beguiling world which a well-bred woman offers to a man opened on Angelito for the first time.

"I thought you meant some special person," said the bullfighter simply.

She lifted her brows. "Oh, did you—whom?"

The *torero* then saw that she did mean some special person and also that this *señorita* was actually willing to be friendly with him and please him. He suddenly felt that he was lifted where he had always longed to be, on a comradely footing with these *señoritas* who came every Sunday to watch him fight. His heart began to beat. Likewise her implication was heady. He knew very well whom she was talking about.

"The trouble is," explained Angelito earnestly, "that you may be brave at the wrong time and cause some one to be angry at you whom you would not have angered for your life!"

The Señorita Miraflores flung up her hands. "A *torero* say such a thing! *Caramba,* you've spoiled all my pleasure in bullfights. I will always think, 'There stands a man who wouldn't dare face that bull if he thought there was the least chance of his getting hurt, not for his life'!"

"But I am not talking about bulls!" cried Angelito. "I am talking about *señoritas!*"

"*Señoritas!* We were talking about herons!"

The bullfighter did not know quite what to say to the laughing girl, but she rescued him good-naturedly by asking him why he grew only guavas and tamarinds in his garden.

In his relief he said unsuspectingly, "My *madre* makes them into jellies and preserves, Señorita."

"Your *madre!*" The *señorita* glanced at him quickly, and then when she saw Angelito's increased embarrassment, she added casually, "I am sure she makes delightful jellies, Señor Angelito."

"You must have some," cried the *torero* with the Spanish impulse to offer anything his guest admires.

"I couldn't think of accepting such a gift."

"Really," pursued Angelito out of his natural generosity, "you must eat a dinner here in the *casa*."

She smiled at him. "Alone, Señor Angelito? I am afraid it is not proper for me to be talking with you alone here in the garden."

The host saw what she meant and paused at the audacity of the idea. "I wonder if the Señora and the Señorita Jiminez . . ." He broke off questioning her mutely.

"Remember your heron!" she laughed.

"Do you really think so?" cried Angelito. "Why, she almost never speaks to me."

The Señorita Miraflores became grave enough. "I am afraid she has a right to be angry, Señor Angelito; you carried him his rapier and clothes, and now . . ." She nodded toward the *casa*.

"Is that it?" cried Angelito with a sudden internal sinking. *"Ehue!* I am afraid I am to blame, I ought never to have allowed him to . . ." He broke off and after a moment added in extenuation, "Still Rafael asked me to get his things."

"Caramba!" snapped Margherita with a woman's instinct not to make the slightest allowance for masculine conventions. "Don't speak of that, I did all I could to prevent him, so should you have, but let's not mention that. Why should you ruin our conversation by mentioning something that is irrevocable?"

"I'm such a blunderer," admitted the fighter.

Came a pause, then Margherita said more evenly, "She really did like your little donkey with. the flowers; she said it made a picture."

"Did she like it?" cried Angelito in great relief.

"God's blood, but after I brought in that donkey how I suffered. 'Ah, Angelito,' I said to myself, 'nobody but a donkey himself would think of bringing a donkey into his *casa!*'"

Margherita burst out laughing. "*Cá!* you were wrong there. Your donkey was a great success and I am very sure she would enjoy some of your *madre's* tamarinds. At any rate she will have to eat them. She can't stay under your roof, Señor, and refuse a meal. No matter what she thinks she can't do that."

Angelito was tempted here to protest his innocence in the wounding of Rafael once more, but remembered he must not introduce the topic. He said he would ask the Jiminezes to a dinner, but if they disliked him he would regret to force them to eat with him out of mere courtesy. Then from some of his endless musings about Socorro Jiminez he suddenly added this quotation, "But, Señorita, to see the Señorita Socorro at my table just once would light a candle in my heart which would still burn when I lie in my shroud."

Señorita Margherita threw up her hands, "*Ola,* what a man!" She turned and ran laughing out of the garden into the *casa.*

This little episode led to the dinner invitation

some two days later. Once he had made up his mind to it, Angelito went about it with a strong attack. One day after he had inquired about Rafael he turned to the ladies in the room. *"Caramba,* Señora, Señoritas!" he exclaimed with the courage that comes with an ordeal. "It is impossible for you to stay in my *casa* and never grace my poor table with your presence; if you will do me the honor of dining with me to-morrow evening . . . "

Margherita immediately accepted for her part and the others had no other choice left them.

After Angelito had gone the ladies sat a little blankly in the chamber with the frieze of rose vases, the crossed rapiers and religious chromos. "Rafael," said the Señora, "this is still another instance of the episodes your egregious bullfighting leads to."

Rafael lay watching the little comedy with weak, amused eyes.

"Cá! Madre, now is the time for you to display your Christian fortitude."

"Fortitude?" repeated the dowager in her baritone voice, suspecting some sort of jest.

"Ciertamente. If one doesn't have charity one at least can have fortitude."

"Brother," said Socorro, "it isn't very respectful to speak to *Maman* like that."

"I meant nothing. . . . "

"*Ay de mi,*" sighed the dowager, "let him jest, Socorro. I don't understand Rafael, I never did."

"He means something about everybody being equal; he is a democrat, *Maman.*"

"I'm sure I don't understand a word of such nonsense—every one equal. That comes of writing poetry all the time. Of course I understand poetry. A poet must say something new, and since the old poets have already said all the sensible things, there is nothing left for a new poet to do but to hatch out absurdities, such as peons are the equal of aristocrats, or that one should be gored by a bull to broaden one's vision."

The Señorita Miraflores rippled into her soft laughter at this, leaned over the bed, and pinched Rafael's finger.

At this point there came a ring at the bell and a little later Señor Montauban entered. He was immediately appealed to and stood drawing off his gloves and listening with his slightly bald head tipped to one side. He addressed his answer mainly to Socorro, with the gravity of a man trying to be brilliant before his sweetheart.

"That is the old conflict between theory and practice," he suggested. "The theory of human equality is very beautiful and it may be true in some abstract way, but life itself is too intimate and personal for us to apply such standards. Our ideals, *Maman*," he turned to the dowager, "are very little more than the excellencies which life suggests but never realizes. They are what the best of our race wish; they are products of the heart, not the head."

The dowager turned to her son. "Now that is clear, Rafael. Why don't you put such ideas as those into your poetry? I never ask Narciso a question but what he explains everything to me precisely as I thought it would be."

"Do you take your religion on the same terms, *madre?*" inquired Rafael as he lay smiling with his eyes shut.

"Now, *hijo*, you know I won't allow you to philosophize about religion in my presence."

"What started such a discussion?" smiled Señor Montauban, glancing at Socorro.

Señorita Miraflores answered. "Angelito invited us all to a dinner and we have accepted. That started us talking about equality."

Señor Montauban nodded. *"Pues*, that ought not to be without interest." He dismissed the topic and turned to the sick man. "Rafael, did you ever complete that manuscript on 'The Gate'?"

"Yes, Socorro copied it for me." He lifted his head to look. "Where is it, sister?"

As the Señorita Jiminez arose to get Rafael's poem, the editor asked: "I don't know whether to mention it or not after Rafael's near tragedy. But, Señora, do you and Socorro want to go to the *corrida* Sunday afternoon, and you will come along with us, too, Margherita? I want to fill the press box with beauty."

"Of course I want to go," cried Margherita, "but we must consider appearances." She leaned over her fiancé again and pulled at his finger. "How do you think it would look, Rafael, for me to go off to see a bullfight just after you have been gored?"

"I!" ejaculated Rafael faintly, opening his eyes. "I think it would look very natural."

The dowager looked at her son suspiciously. "I never know exactly how to take you, Rafael—natural, what do you mean by natural?"

"Why, *Maman*, he means natural!" Margherita was very pleased. "So we will go, Socorro. Rafael is nearly well."

The Señorita Jiminez at the other end of the room let drop a fascicle of paper.

"*Pues*, yes," she agreed in a queer voice, "I suppose we might as well go . . ." Her voice trailed out in indecision and her glance wandered up to the rapiers crossed on the wall.

No sooner had Angelito left the sick room than he fell into uneasiness about the conduct of the dinner which he had planned.

"Sangre de Dios!" he thought to himself. "That was a rash thing for me to do. There are a great many points in giving a dinner to aristocrats which I know little about. . . ."

He walked on down the *patio* toward his mother's room meditating the uncertainties of his adventure. He paused on the way down to look into his dining room on the right side of the *patio*. A notion flitted through his head that he should order a profusion of flowers, but this was dismissed.

When the bullfighter entered his mother's room he found old Ana handing a lottery ticket through her window to some customer in the street outside. The bullfighter was instantly irritated. He watched in silence as the old peon woman ran a hand into a skirt pocket, drew out a handful of beggarly copper coins and placed the ticket and the change into the hand stretched into the window. Not until the deal

was finished did she see Angelito; then she gave a
faint start, and immediately her old face took on its
obstinate expression.

The *torero* made no comment but said in a flat
voice that told he was angry, *"Madre,* I wish you
would prepare a dinner for to-morrow night."

The old woman lost her mulish expression in surprise at this tack. "Don't you get a dinner every
night, Pancho?"

"Seguro," his voice still showing his vexation,
"but to-morrow night I have company."

"Who?" asked old Ana suspiciously.

"Pues, the Señora and the Señoritas in the front
room."

"Diabolo!" cried the old peon. "Those cats—why
did you invite them?"

"Cá! They were here in my *casa!"*

"Here in your *casa! Diantre,* yes, and they go
about without so much as glancing at you. You
might be a thousand miles away. They never see
you and in your own *casa,* too. But you stand
twisting your head after her as if she was a processional in the cathedral! Pancho, you are the big-
gest fool I ever saw!"

"Oh, la! la! There is no use running on like
that. Will you cook the dinner?"

"No, I will not!"

Angelito looked at his mother in frustration. She looked like a kind of ugly human post driven down in his path to keep him from advancing a step. "*Entonces*," he snapped, "I will go down to La India and buy a dinner!"

"What? Buy a dinner! *Absoluto*, Pancho, you are gone mad indeed over this wench. Whoever heard of buying a dinner!"

"It is you who drive me to madness," declared Angelito somberly; "you refusing me this little dinner when I have to fight in the *circo* the day after to-morrow. *Ola*, who knows what will happen the day after to-morrow! You might think of that before you refused me a little dinner for a few friends."

The old crone stood looking at the bullfighter for several minutes and her face slowly changed. She made a despairing gesture, "*Ay Maria*, Pancho, somehow we always manage to break each other's hearts. God in Heaven knows I wish you would give up this bullfighting. You have enough money, but if you should marry this white-faced *bicho*, then, *seguro*, your fighting will never end. All she would want would be the money you could give her. If she really loved you, Pancho, she could not endure to see you enter the *circo*. Holy Virgin, she would rather cut off her hand than to see you do so terrible a thing!"

Angelito had hoped to bring about some such re-action as this.

"Then you will make the dinner?" he asked in a kinder voice.

"*Sí, sí!*"

He pondered a moment. "We will need some plates and silver, *madre*."

"Plates and silver! We have always eaten out of plates, Pancho, and we have knives and forks and spoons."

"*Sí*, but I have been thinking of getting something for my table for a long time, *madre*. It is absurd in a great *casa* like this to have no plates and silver."

"But, Pancho, you will make a beggar of your-self!"

"*Cá*, no," declared the bullfighter pleased at hav-ing introduced the topic so deftly. "A single fight will make all the money back and more too. I won-der what I should have carved on my silver?"

"What do you carve on silver?"

"Oh, a crest, a motto, a figure, a shield, one's ini-tials . . ."

The old woman looked at him shrewdly and then

lowered her voice, "Are you afraid they will steal it, Pancho?"

"*Huy!* No!" The son was disgusted. "It is a family mark, something the father of a great family puts on his plate to pass down to his sons and grandsons. It is a little sign, *madre,* carved on one's plate to show that life does not end with one *caballero,* but it marches through him to his sons and through them to his grandsons, and so on and on, like a soldier marching to war. It is not he, nor is it they, *madre,* but it is an invincible immortal something which becomes him and them for a space and passes on. And only *caballeros* have it."

The old peon shook her head at her son. "I am sure I don't know what you mean, Pancho, and I don't think you do either."

From this triumph over his mother Angelito hurried down to a jewelry store on Plaza Bolivar to purchase his family plate. The jeweler was a fat saddle-colored man with a polished black mustache and an unctious manner. He showed the bullfighter design after design, some from Madrid, some from Paris, some of an English make from Birmingham.

Angelito chose his plate in a Spanish style and then explained to the proprietor of the *joyeria* that he wanted a motto carved on it, an inscription, a something. . . .

At last the jeweler apprehended what the *torero* had in his head and produced an old book on heraldry. Here were an endless number of the vaunting phrases which human beings had chosen to express their flair of life. They were in all languages for the emotion which prompted them is as broad as humanity itself. "Glory and Grief," *"Ad Cielo," "Resurgam," "Verité sans Peur,"* "Honor and King," *"Semper Fidelis,"* and so on, crest after crest, crystallizations of what life had meant for some series of human souls. Angelito chose, after the jeweler had explained the meaning of the phrase, *"Ad Astra per Asper."* (To the Stars through Difficulties.)

The jeweler complimented him on his choice and later smiled as he engraved innumerable "Ad Astra per Asper's" on Angelito's plate.

On the afternon of the next day the tradesman dispatched a porter with a heavy box to the blue *casa* on Traposo. The porter was a peon, in flowing shirt, straw hat, and *alpargatas,* and he meandered along the *calles* with Angelito's family plate rattling in a push cart.

Chapter 6

SEÑOR MONTAUBAN happened to be calling on the Jiminez family when Angelito's dinner was served and the bullfighter conscripted him to the feast. Likewise it became a question whether or not Rafael might be moved in to the table. There was considerable discussion on this point. Rafael's physician was telephoned and at last the poet was wheeled through the *patio* into the *comidor* and instated at the table in a black and yellow silk dressing gown.

They made a gay crowd with Rafael getting better. Angelito sat at the head of the table with the Señora Jiminez on his right and the Señorita Miraflores to his left. Socorro Jiminez and Señor Montauban were taking care of Rafael.

The bullfighter surveyed his guests and his table piled with viands and pleasure vibrated through his breast. After the fashion of peons, the whole meal had been placed on the table at once; roasted chickens heaped with brown rice and garnished with peppers. Around this central dish were boiled yammi in a great white mound on a big dish; then

there was a large bowl of fried plantains, brown and
syrupy. Half gourds of guava jelly, which old Ana
had turned out into finger bowls, glowed like
topazes under the electric spray overhead. Tamarind preserves were in a ewer. At each plate lay
one knife, one fork, and one spoon, which were
clearly meant for continuous service. And all the
silver was fire new with the burr from the engraver's
burin still roughening the "Ad astra per asper's"
with which it was marked.

"To the stars through difficulties." Well, Angelito had reached the stars at last. The glitter of
his silver, the gleam of his china which he had received that afternoon, were tiny fires which warmed
his heart with the delight of new possession. And
above the abundance and shine of his feast he saw
the disturbing charm of Señorita Jiminez.

It was odd how the girl moved him. He did not
see her as he did his other guests. In some way
her very appearance seemed to slip away from him
if he withdrew his eyes from her face but for a
moment. This elusive quality forced him to glance
at her again and again. And yet all the rest of the
diners wore the most matter-of-fact aspect; the
comely Señora, the gay and pretty Margherita, the
wan and handsome poet in his black and yellow

dressing gown, and the dapper little editor with his slightly bald head.

Now and then Angelito interrupted the conversation of his guests to press them to take more food. Old Ana moved about the table keeping the wine glasses filled. The sprightly Margherita was telling with much humor of her flight from the heron in the garden.

Socorro Jiminez said she had not known the *casa* had a garden and asked if it had any orchids, and began describing a very rare blue orchid which Rafael had brought back from the upper reaches of the Orinoco.

The girl's observation seemed to Angelito to be of the greatest moment. He assured her earnestly that there was a little garden in the rear of his *casa,* but it was a badly neglected spot, overgrown with wild guavas and a tamarind tree.

"And these tamarind preserves came off of it," interposed Margherita; "Señor Angel's mother made them."

"Señor Angel's mother!" echoed the Señora.

There was a little talk of the *torero's* mother. This made Angelito exquisitely uncomfortable, and he said vaguely that his mother was very old, and that he carried the tamarinds to her."

"What amazes me," said Socorro, glancing about with her dark eyes, "is this *casa*, the garden, this *comidor* in which we sit, the food we are eating is all founded on bullfighting. Now isn't that strange! Just think, I am sitting here because Señor Angel risked his life in the arena. I eat this bit of bread because a charging bull grazed him. We are eating danger."

"*Cá*, Socorro," said the Señora in her deep voice, "it is an art. It is as if he had won his *casa* by painting pictures."

"He does paint pictures," declared Rafael, "the most luminous and dramatic pictures in the whole world. Sorolla can never get the brilliancy of a scene in the amphitheater."

"His pictures don't last very long," giggled Margherita.

"Brevity is their virtue," asserted Rafael with more earnestness than his weakness justified.

"*Pues,* Rafael, that is a defect," said the dowager; "one can't study it."

"That is the point," declared the poet; "the response to beauty is an emotion. If one stops to study it, you intellectualize it and your emotion vanishes. It is the evanescence of beauty that gives it worth. That is what gives all life its sense of pathos and sweetness. Look at Margherita. Would she wring my heart with tenderness if she could never fade? Nobody could feel tenderness for an immortal being. Such a sentiment would be inappropriate. It would be like kissing the Rock of Gibraltar."

"*Caramba, mamān*," cried Margherita, "what a boy you have reared. He is impossible."

"Rafael," returned the dowager gravely, "you must remember that all of us are immortal, and now we will cease discussing any such topic."

"We were talking about bullfights," said Socorro, "when Rafael refused to kiss Gibraltar. I think I am getting opposed to bullfights myself. There is a political party in Spain trying to abolish it over there isn't there?"

"But they never will," declared Señor Montauban with the ardor of a devotee. "The bullfight epitomizes the Spanish spirit. It avoids the mere brutal pain and dull security of pugilism. *Caramba*, I've wondered why the English and American pugilists don't take thumb and forefinger and squeeze each other's noses until one cried 'enough.' That would not be any more undignified than beating each other with their fists and the sport would then be entirely devoid of danger."

"But what's the use of danger?" asked Margherita impatiently. "I think it's awful; think of Rafael risking his life in a *capeas!*"

"Danger," explained the editor smoothly, "prevents a moral and intellectual stagnation in an individual or a nation."

"I am sure danger wouldn't make me any better or brighter," declared Margherita.

"It wouldn't? If you thought you were in danger now, you have no idea how swiftly your wits would begin to work. It would stir you up. And all peoples have emotional depths which must be sounded at intervals if they are to progress in the world. When a nation comes face to face with danger or death it purifies the national mind of trifles like the surge of a great black sea. That is why war, Señorita, is always followed by a great renaissance, a reorientation of spirit."

"What has that to do with bullfighting?" inquired the Señora.

"Everything. War is wasteful, Señora. The sacrifice of life and wealth is too great. We Spanish people have found a more economical mode of purging our souls in the swift and actual danger of the *circo*. Because we have the bullfight it is not necessary for Spanish nations to go to war. North

America has her substitute in football which kills a certain number of her young men every year, but football lacks two great philosophic factors which the bullfight possesses."

The editor paused here for the Señora to ask what those two factors were.

"One is sincerity. The North American football players cannot sincerely strive to kill their rivals, and this lowers the whole world of football to the triviality of a game. No great nation can thrive on trivialities in a matter touching their profoundest moral needs. The other objection is that the opponent of a football player is human and of about equal strength with himself. This destroys the profound antithesis between man and nature which finds its most complete symbol in tauromachy. In the *circo*, the bull represents the prodigious forces of nature, vast, furious, and brutal. The bull is as devoid of moral qualms as a cyclone or an earthquake. Pitted against this immense violence stands a man entirely without passion, trusting his life to his precision, coolness and judgment. Señora, Señoritas, that is the very graph of all human existence. We stand every moment of our lives opposed to terrific and brutal forces. Because the national sport of the Spanish peoples is the sincere

battle to death between a bull and a man, the whole
Spanish race finds itself more at home in the world
than do less favored nations. Our philosophers
look upon life with sincerer eyes; our artists see
life and color more truly; our writers present life
more frankly than do the equivocating novelists of
the northern countries. Indeed, if I may say it,
the two powerful cathartics which keep the Spanish
soul free from all pettiness, worldliness, hypocrisy
and stagnation are our Holy Church and the bullfight. You, Señor Angel, are as truly a high priest
in the service of God as the bishop before the altar.
You perform the ancient rite of sprinkling blood
upon the sand, whereas the priest uses merely the
symbol of blood, water."

Señor Montauban delivered his peroration with
great energy and seized his glass of wine to drink
to Angelito and the profession of tauromachy when
old Ana, who was standing behind Margherita,
burst out, "Holy Virgin, listen to that dried up
little mango seed clattering away about what a fine
thing it is to get killed when he's safe enough in
the boxes. *Demonio*, you don't risk your hide,
Señor, for the sake of your soul, or for anybody
else's soul. You don't . . ."

All the diners turned at this extraordinary outbreak from the serving woman. The editor got to his feet.

"Señor," he cried to Angelito, "do you allow your servants to insult your guests?"

The bullfighter was beside himself. "Three thousand devils on horseback!" he shouted. "*Madr*—Ana, what do you mean interrupting my guests!"

"I mean he is putting you up to fight more bulls —bah—a shriveled little toad like him!"

"Get out of here! Go!" cried the *torero*, growing dark with rage.

The old peon woman suddenly flung out her arms, "Oh, what madness this is! This will lead to some terrible thing! No good can come of this! And you," she flared out at the editor again, "saying that a bullfighter is as holy as the bishop, you will fry in hell for that, you wicked aristocrat!"

The contumacious old crone turned and moved out of the *comidor*, waggling her head obstinately and leaving the guests in confusion.

Angelito had a dizzy sensation as if he were sinking in space. His guests were arising from their places, and he mechanically followed their example. They came around saying things to him which he did not clearly follow. The Señora was saying in her baritone something about the insolence of servants these days. The bullfighter was apologizing incoherently to the editor. Then Angelito saw them go slowly out of his *comidor,* rolling Rafael in their midst.

Presently the *torero* was standing alone in his dining room. His new china and silverware twinkled at him under the electric spray. On the shaft of a silver ladle his eyes caught the newly engraved inscription, which was to be the motto of his house, "Ad Astra per Asper."

When the Jiminezes had retired to their room, and after Señor Montauban had made his adieus to them, the editor succeeded in getting a moment alone with Socorro in the entry of the *casa.* He drew her to him and kissed her with the passion small men feel for large women. As he did so he murmured the conventional Spanish endearments, *"mi alma . . . pequena cielo,"* although he could hardly call her *"pequena"* since she was a trifle taller than he and must have weighed more.

"You are prepossessed to-night," he observed presently, *"Cá!* That scene was enough to give any one a disagreeable farewell. It is my theory,

Socorro, that a real servant is impossible unless
there is a clearcut line of social demarkation between the master and the servant. Otherwise a
man does not have a servant at all, but a boorish
companion."

Socorro Jiminez, who stood with her hand on her
fiancé's lapel, thought to herself, "That is true—
Narciso has a very clever head. I wonder why I
don't appreciate him more highly. Everything he
says is interesting. Perhaps we have been be-
trothed too long." A moment later when he took
his leave she submitted to his fervent embrace and
bent her head a trifle to his kiss. She caught a
faint agreeable odor of fine cigars. He gave her
waist and torso a little extra pressure, "What are
you thinking about?" he asked in a pettish tone.

"Nothing—I suppose this is a reaction from the
strain of nursing Rafael."

"Yes, yes," he agreed more gently. He took her
hand, held it until he was at her arm's length, then
touched his lips to it. "I'll be glad when you are
back in your home and these pretty fingers can
make me some music, Socorro."

"Yes, it's been a siege here."

"*Hasta, mañana.*"

"*Adios, pues.*"

Señor Montauban let himself out of the small panel in the big double entrance, and then Socorro could hear his small feet tapping briskly down the *calle*.

The young woman stood for several moments in the entry, oppressed by a vague heavy feeling. When she returned slowly to the sick room she glanced out into the *patio* and saw the whole back part of the *casa* was darkened. This increased her melancholy and she did not know why.

When she reached the sick room she found Margherita angry and her mother very dignified toward Rafael who was in bed again.

The Señorita Miraflores turned sharply to her future sister-in-law. "Rafael," she began accusingly, "says all that food piled up on the table wasn't a display of bad taste and lack of refinement. Why you know it was, Socorro. It took my appetite completely, and the silver—" She broke out laughing in the midst of her pique, "every single piece used wrong. I had to think up a funny story I knew and tell it to Señor Angel so I would have a reason to laugh."

"I say," explained Rafael soberly, "if the sight of a large amount of food takes Margherita's appetite, the trouble lies with her."

"I say peons make a banquet by piling on a lot of food and nice people by serving a little at a time!" cried Margherita, angry again.

"And why?" demanded Rafael lifting himself on his elbow. "Simply because we 'nice' people, as you call us, have lost our simplicity. We have overstuffed and underworked ourselves. Why should the sight of a great deal of food be repellent unless we have had some painful experience with much food. Our likes and dislikes are based on something. They don't just happen. So instead of a piled-up plate looking piggish, the person who can't stand a piled-up plate simply has been piggish, and he advertises his surfeit by asking for a very little at a time—like a sick man. That's what you call refinement, Margherita—having been a pig."

Margherita was on the verge of tears.

"Oh, don't argue with him, Margherita," advised the Señora; "let him turn everything around. He does it to show how bright he is."

"But, *Maman,* everything he says is so *silly!*"

The dowager rolled her comely head in acquiescence. "Men are like that, Margherita; his father was, he is, Señor Montauban is more or less, though not so bad as Rafael. What Narciso was saying about priests and bullfighters, shameful! I thought that old woman, Ana, was almost right. Socorro, my dear, you are going to have a lot to put up with when you are mistress of the Montauban château."

"Look at money," proceeded Rafael, who, manlike, could not forsake his argument. "Nobody considers great piles of money in bad taste, simply because money has never made any one physically sick, although it has made many a man mentally sick, I'll warrant, but our emotions are not based on reason but on our physical senses."

"We were talking about food, not money!" snapped Margherita. "That's just like you, Rafael, you *always* jump the track."

Rafael eased himself back down in bed. He looked across at the women with the quirked lips and half-closed eyes of a man disgusted by feminine stupidity. He thought to himself, "Why do I ever speak a serious word to these women!" As he looked at Margherita she seemed a kind of pouting emptiness. "I won't talk to them any more," he thought; "it is like quarreling with children."

"I have no sympathy for Señor Angel either," stated Socorro, who in some way had shifted the point at issue from the table to the host, "not a bit. He is the one who really caused Rafael to get hurt. And then, after he did it, he brought Rafael here instead of taking him properly to his own home, so I haven't a bit of sympathy for him, none whatever!"

As she hotly insisted that she had no sympathy whatever, tears moistened Socorro's eyes and a curious quiver flickered through her chest as though she were about to sob.

"Why, he didn't do it!" cried Rafael, flaring up in his friend's behalf again. "I made him bring me here, and as for causing me to get wounded, he flung himself on the bull's head and saved my life by risking his own. I was right down under the brute, when Angelito leaped on it bodily. The bull charged half way across the arena with Angelito wedged in between its horns before he stabbed it in the head and killed it.

Margherita said, "Well, he got you into it, it was his duty to get you out."

"Got me into it! Ten thousand devils, Margherita, will I never become an autonomous human being? I tell you he tried to dissuade me from entering the *corrida!* He opposed every step I took, even down to the particular bull I fought, and now you say he got me into it, *Demonio!*"

The sick man turned his face to the wall and thought irritably, "These imbeciles! And I am going to have to live out my life with that little fool! Sacred fiends of Hell!"

Socorro Jiminez was so disturbed at this account that she could not trust herself to say more. She bade her family good night and started through the *patio* to her own bedchamber. As she passed through the colonnade the darkness in the back of the *casa* intensified the sadness of her mood. In this darkness the pitifulness of Señor Angel's dinner, the misconduct of his servant, his mistakes in serving food and using his silver, all filled her with an intense pathos. And topping all this came the revelation that Señor Angel had risked his life for her brother. The girl fumbled for her handkerchief and wiped away the tears which she could feel wetting her eyelids. It seemed to her that never before in all her life had she loved her brother so tenderly or so intensely.

Chapter 7

On the following day the physician agreed that Rafael was sufficiently recovered to be removed to the Jiminez villa. That morning the Señora Jiminez bade Angelito farewell and expressed her gratitude for his many kindnesses with such cold formality that it quite precluded any further intercourse between her family and the *torero*. The Señorita Margherita told him gaily that she would see him in the *circo* Sunday afternoon. The Señorita Socorro shook hands with the bullfighter, said how kind he had been, and the impression that remained with her longest was the pressure of his hard, rubbery hand over her own. It hurt her faintly, doubling the soft cartilage in her palm and left pink finger marks on the back of her hand. After she was in the cab with Rafael and her mother driving home, she had an illusion that her hand was still in the hard fingers of the *torero* and once or twice she glanced down at the imprints he had left.

When Socorro had settled herself once more in

the sunshiny villa, Angelito and the whole bull-fighting world which had risen up about her in the blue *casa* in such intimate fashion now sank back and became a part of that obscure underworld of work folk whose labor, skill, and hazards supplied Paraiso with all the necessities, pleasures, and diversions of its life. Socorro Jiminez, like all the rest of her class, thought little or nothing about this work world. She knew, of course, everything that made life pleasant to her did this nether plane furnish, but she had an impression that these working people were created expressly to administer to her own group, the aristocratic group, and that this aristocratic group formed the real substance of Caracan life; and all the rest, the bakers, truckers, tailors, *toreros*, and what not, were merely the underpinning which served to support this precious and significant minority of artistocrats. Naturally among those who slumped into this ancillary world was the bullfighter, Angelito.

Thus Socorro's home-coming dehumanized the very human and troubled world which she found in the blue *casa* on Traposo *calle*. Angelito was, after all, a bullfighter, a handsomely built man who supported a rather expensive *casa* by the extraordinary method of fighting bulls. It was a queer way to make a living. In fact, Socorro had the South American feeling that to *make* a living was queer and, to be frank, rather gross. One should live on the rentals of an estate on the Tuy or some such inconspicuous source of income which one had inherited.

After Socorro had returned to her home, Señor Montauban visited the Jiminezes daily as he had been doing for a long time. He listened to Socorro's piano playing, complimented her technical excellence, and compared her with Venezuela's great pianiste, Carrena, with whom he was personally acquainted.

The Señorita Jiminez esteemed her fiancé as rather a clever musical critic, for he was always attentive to the actual notes which she produced. He would sit for half an hour at a time, seldom longer than that for he tired quickly, parsing the grammar of her musical phrases.

"No, Socorro," he would say, "a little more limpidity here, *mi alma*," and he would walk over to the keyboard and tap out the notes, for he played a little himself. Or, "that *cadenza* was not quite your usual string of pearls, *mi vida*," and he would show her on the score precisely which string of pearls he was talking about.

The Señorita Jiminez always felt flattered if she escaped with only one or two such criticisms, yet somehow they annoyed her, and frustrated her. She felt he was never listening to the music, but to her notes. He would stop her right in the midst of a performance to correct a defect. The real pleasure the editor derived from her performance came from this attitude of critical superiority which he always assumed. The musical staff was to Señor Montauban so many parallel bars upon which he performed critical gymnastics; further than this music appeared to him unnecessary.

Socorro, on the whole, was fond of Señor Montauban. His slightly bald head looked distinguished to her. She often said to him, and rather believed it, "Nearly all intellectual men are a little bald, Narciso." She liked his philosophizings better than she did Rafael's. They were more matter of fact and not so badly timed. To move a woman philosophy must be as accurately timed as the ignition of a twelve-cylinder car. Montauban felt this. In fact, his mind had a practical, finical cast which the girl found as congenial as the mind of another woman. One objection to him was his occasional gusts of surreptitious kisses and embraces. However, Socorro pondered that no lover was perfect. And then, after all, his little bursts of amorousness seemed not so objectionable as unnecessary.

One day, in the midst of one of these outbursts, the girl questioned its good taste and said it reminded her of peons. The editor loosed her abruptly and began a dissertation on the essential oneness of human emotions. "The difference between persons," he said, "is mental, not emotional. Upon just such *siroccos* is founded the whole Spanish civilization." He chose to call them *"siroccos."* "And to question their essential dignity, or even their sacramental character, is to undermine the very foundations of society, and indeed of all life." This interview left Socorro considerably chastened and she made no further outspoken comments on what resembled what. After all, it is a poor wit who cannot defend his own prerogatives against the undisciplined attack of a girl. There is now little doubt among the anthropologists that logic first appeared on this earth through some baldheaded cave man reading the riot act to some cave maiden about her social obligations.

The Sunday afternoon following Rafael's removal to his home found the invalid well enough to be left with the servants in the villa while the Señora

and the Señorita Jiminez and Señorita Miraflores
went with Señor Montauban to the bullfight.

By this time Socorro's complacent world had
completely reoriented itself, and Angelito had vanished from it. Socorro and the other ladies walked
down to the gate where stood the editor's motor
and as she established herself in the front seat beside Narciso, who drove his own car, she was filled
with a sense of well-being.

The big car glided silently down the boulevard
through the shade of tropical trees. Occasionally
Socorro got a whiff of the editor's aromatic cigar.
In the rear seat the Señora and Margherita were
talking, and now and then Socorro caught an occasional word such as "jade cabochon" or "silver
sequins." The editor was telling Socorro something
about Tito Monnico's new mural in Bolivar's *casa*.
The girl listened not very attentively, but it
pleased her for Narciso to talk about pictures in
such a sophisticated manner. He was a brilliant
man and he would make a brilliant and very desirable husband. He was driving his car with his hat
off and it seemed to her that he never looked more
distinguished. His features were fairly regular and
finely carved. His hands on the wheel, one gloved
and one ungloved, were small yet muscular look-

ing. The thought flickered through her head, and warmed her face somewhat, that their children, she meant to have four, would be beautiful.

The municipal band was playing in Bolivar plaza as the big shining car nosed carefully around the crowded square on the way to the *circo*. The strains of music, the colorful crowd, the many salutes and hat tippings which Señor Montauban and his party received from both sides, all formed a part of a pleasing deference which Socorro felt doubly due her as a present Jiminez and a prospective Montauban.

A little farther east they passed the low but massive cathedral and a priest standing in the recessed doorway lifted his little round hat at the motor. Señor Montauban eased the car to a murmuring halt.

"Do you go to the *circo*, Father Ignacio?" he asked across the narrow pavement.

Father Ignacio had the look of an athletic man gone to fat. His face was a wrinkled bronze. He bowed a *"gracias"* and came across the pavement smiling as Margherita opened the rear door and made room.

"Yes, I am to hold prayers for the *toreros*," he

nodded, extending a hand to the women which Margherita kissed. "I am afraid the *circo* will not be well attended to-day." His voice, which rumbled like an orator's, held a regret that any function which he blessed would not be well attended.

"You could hardly expect it," agreed Señor Montauban, starting the car again, "with the Spanish *corrida* right upon us. The people are saving their *soldes* to get into that."

"Who do you think will be second *espada* to Juan Leon, Señor Montauban?" inquired the priest with a deference due the editor of the single paper in Caracas devoted entirely to the sport of bullfighting.

"I know whom I am going to support through the pages of '*Sol y Sombra*'."

"Ercolito?" inquired the priest.

A little stab went through Socorro at such a suggestion. She turned in her seat to face the father.

"No, *padre,* not Ercolito, Angelito!"

The priest smiled, "You seem very earnest, daughter."

The Señora Jiminez explained that "this Angelito," such were the words she used to describe the fighter, "this Angelito" had done her dear

Rafael a great service and the whole family felt most grateful to him and would be glad to see him get the post of honor.

"I am glad you mentioned this," said the priest good naturedly. "It happens I know Señor Malestar, and if the topic comes up between us, I will suggest that he use Angelito as second *espada*."

Socorro thanked the father impulsively and promised him a donation for the repair of the cathedral roof which at the time was the object of alms.

A few moments later the automobile turned out of the narrow *calle* into the sun-shot plaza before the bull ring. The ring itself was a great, red, circular structure, made of brick and finished in front like a castle. Beyond this gloomily ornamented façade the high walls curved away as featureless as the walls of a prison. They were high, blank, and red, without a variation in the brick masonry to break their monotonous curve. The *circo* always gave Socorro a heavy brutal impression.

The motor was parked a little distance from the castle-like entrance. Señor Montauban, who held a press pass, did not visit the ticket window where a little queue of *aficionados* stood in the sunshine, but led his little party straight into the wide entrance where an ascending platform led up to the

level of the boxes. After climbing this, the party
came out on an immense concrete oval which held
a scattering of spectators in its innumerable boxes.
As Socorro followed Señor Montauban around a
long walkway behind the boxes and in front of the
ordinary ascending tiers of seats, a number of
acquaintances bowed to the party. Once Señor
Montauban paused to shake the hand of some gov-
ernmental official.

"A very poor attendance, Dr. Sanchez," said
Montauban, glancing about the huge circle of
empty boxes.

"It is the *hors d'œuvre* before the *plat du jour*,"
smiled the doctor, referring to the coming Spanish
corrida, "but in this sport, Señor Montauban, one
doesn't dare miss anything."

"*Bueno! Bueno!*" Montauban proceeded down
the aisle to his own box, smiling. It always pleased
him for any one to praise the art of bullfighting.

Notwithstanding the smallness of the attendance,
everybody was in spirits at the approaching bullfight. Amid this general expectation and pleasure
Socorro Jiminez found her share. The press box
which Señor Montauban occupied was exactly in
the center of the "*sombra*" side of the *circo*. Some
ten feet below the balustrade of the box was the

runway for the attendants of the bullring; this in turn was fenced off by barriers from the great yellow arena. At the southern end of the ring the bull pens and the dressing room for the fighters had been housed under an immense proscenium for motion pictures. This huge structure was used when some very popular cinema was brought to Caracas.

The press box occupied the best position in the great edifice and this fact renewed Socorro Jiminez's luxurious feeling of being well placed in life. All things gave her a sense of quiet pleasure; the bright yellow light which swept the amphitheater and which was reflected from the opposite or *"sol"* side of the circle; a cool breeze that breathed down from the mountains over the boxes; the color and gaiety of the few spectators. She was indeed very well placed in life. Her family, her social position, her future career as the Señora Montauban were perfectly assured. All she had to do simply was to live and enjoy all these prerogatives, the music, the spectacle, the clothes, the very feel of her own beautifully molded body. She was a very happy girl, or at least she ought to be one.

The band broke suddenly into music, one of Yriade's sensuous and intricate nocturnes. It was not badly played. The tendrils of the *aria* immediately wound themselves around the girl's mood, rendering it pensive and sweeter. Like all Spanish music it was intense gaiety based on sadness. In the orchestration were innumerable gay sparkling effects, but its basic movement was passionate and sad. It recalled to Socorro what Rafael had said about tragedy and death at Angelito's unfortunate dinner. She sat trying to recall just his words when she felt Narciso's touch on her hand. She gave him a little impulsive pressure in return, but he was leaning toward her to say that he did not care for Yriade's melodramatic effects. He was surprised at the conductor of the municipal band for selecting such music. He preferred the restraint of the classics.

Socorro felt faintly reproved for enjoying the music. It seemed to her that Narciso must be a very brilliant man indeed, perpetually intellectual, cool and critical . . . she was a little relieved when he took back his hand and allowed her once more to relapse into the rhythm and melancholy of the music.

Just as its mood suffused her once more, it ceased. Came a little interval of silence, then the band broke forth in a military march. The southern doors of the arena opened and in came the parade of the fighters.

They made a brilliant spectacle as they marched around the arena. Socorro leaned forward gazing at them when presently she picked out Angelito at the head of the procession. She breathed a trifle faster and became conscious of a faint nervous play through her chest. His brilliant regalia gave him a strange look which rather pleased the girl. She was pleased at this change from his commonplace home wear. She had forgotten how resplendent he was in the bullring.

The train of men, *toreros, banderilleros, monosabios,* the two black mules with their bright harness forming the tail of the queue, made a colorful procession against the yellow sunlit wall on the opposite side of the amphitheater. They gleamed and glowed like a peal of bold music. They were so unafraid. They actually were going to risk their lives as did poor Rafael. Her brother's accident had deepened a *corrida* for the girl, it had changed it from a spectacle into a very solid and dangerous reality. Her eyes returned fascinated to the unfamiliar figure of Angelito; the bold way he walked and swung his cloak. And his demeanor had seemed so repressed, even constrained, in the

blue *casa.* She recalled the fiasco of his dinner
and his darkened *patio* after his servant had ruined
his feast. But here he was now with rapier and
cloak, about to meet the bulls as gallantly as ever.
That seemed a courageous thing to do. If she had
been shamed by disorderly servants she did not believe she could ever march at the head of a procession again.

She continued watching the *torero* as he came
around the northern arc of the boxes. By this
time he was close enough for her to see his face.
And instantly she knew with a little thrill that he
meant to fling up his cloak on her balustrade. It
gave her a peculiar pleasure to *know* that a *torero*
meant to honor her with his cloak. As he came
still closer she could see that he was looking directly at her.

He was quite different from the silent man she
had seen in the blue *casa.* His black eyes in his
bold swarthy face dealt her a sort of sharp emotional blow. It increased the titillations in her
chest until Socorro hardly knew whether it was
pleasant or unpleasant. She gazed back at him almost perforce. Again it appeared as if she had
never before seen this man, in his brilliant carmine
cloak and his little black *mona* stuck on the back

of his head, this man who had eyes that held hers by some extraordinary power. She had never seen him before. She had not known there was such a man. Her sense of surprise at him and at her own self increased.

Señor Montauban selected this inopportune moment to say that the processional of the fighters always held for him a very medieval atmosphere and that the poetry and romance of the bullfight was exactly this mellowness of time and custom, this. . . .

Without taking her eyes from Angelito, she begged in a breath, "Please don't talk, Narciso, till they get past."

At that moment the bullfighter was right under her box. The wistfulness of his face looking up at her, the bronze column of his neck spreading into powerful shoulders and deep chest, all seemed somehow sharply intimate to Socorro. The very *mona* over his bullfighter's queue took on part and parcel of this intimacy and concern for him. She hoped from the depths of her heart that he would not get hurt in this *corrida*.

At that moment Angelito, still looking at her, swung off his cloak and, with an easy movement, sent it up to her. She reached out impulsively, caught the carmine garment, and the next moment a strong perfume was all about her.

Margherita leaned over and helped her friend spread the rich cloak on the balustrade.

"That's very nice of Señor Angel to honor us," smiled Margherita. "Doesn't he look splendid in that dark red suit?" She leaned farther and murmured privately in her companion's ear, "Did you ever see such powerfully turned calves?" She glanced gaily in Socorro's eyes, and then resumed her conversation with the Señora.

When Angelito flung up his cloak the other players followed his example and the whole oval was decorated with bright splashes of color. The fighters then broke their formation and went running out into the arena to await the entry of the bull.

Socorro leaned over the balustrade watching this familiar phase of the bullfight and nervously smoothing the velvet cloak under her fingers. The strong intimate perfume of the garment rose up about her. It was a mannish odor. It pushed itself not unpleasantly on her attention and it struck her that Señor Montauban never used perfume. Naturally he would not. It was not "nice." As she continued moving her fingers over the cloak the pile of the velvet set up delicate tremors running up into her hands and arms and chest.

The band ceased playing and there came a blast from the trumpeter. Socorro and every one else in the arena leaned forward looking steadily at the bull's entrance. The next moment a door opened under the great proscenium. It was a little black rectangle in the sunlight. Suddenly in it appeared the head and shoulders of a bull. A man on the stage above the opening hurled down two steel-tipped rosettes. The next instant the animal lunged into the arena, leaping high in air and coming down stiff-legged in an effort to jar loose the rosettes.

Instantly the *banderilleros* started running at the bull, flinging out their crimson capes as they went. An instant later the bull charged a man near the center.

Socorro leaned forward and followed this stage of the game intently. A sudden unusual interest in the fight filled her. Then, in the midst of these preliminary passes, a vague premonition of disaster formed in her mind. She was afraid the bull would hurt some of the *aficionados*. She stared at the lunging animal. Its heavy convex neck with its tremendous tossing power appalled her. An upsweep of those horns could destroy any living thing . . .

At every charge of the bull, the girl gripped the bright cloak under her fingers. When a player held out his cape and allowed the huge animal to storm under it, a tingle went through Socorro's body as if some one had struck a harp string in her breast. It seemed to Socorro that something was wrong with her. Never before had she been so moved, so wrought up by mere cape play.

The girl's sense of danger, of imminent tragedy, grew sharper and sharper, as if some one were running a scale on a piano . . . higher and higher. It seemed to Socorro that soon she must come to the limit of her endurance, when there came that pause, that interim after the *banderilleros* have finished playing the bull, and immediately before the *torero* comes out alone to kill it.

This gap in time quivered past, then the wrought-up girl saw a carmine figure advance into the yellow sand. She leaned forward with her lips apart and the arena seemed to swing slightly before her eyes. She breathed short breaths through her open lips. She saw that single gay figure advancing on the bull. That was all she saw. That sight absorbed her eyes, her breath, her nerves. . . .

A great circle of blackness seemed to surround the *torero* and the bull, but in its center these two figures stood out in intense illumination. The carmine figure stamped its foot, swung its scarlet cape; the bull charged. As the bull dashed under the outstretched arms, it seemed as if every cord in Socorro's bosom were struck terrifically. The circle of darkness around man and bull wavered, almost closed. The bull wheeled and was charging again. The man either was or was not stepping aside. The vacillating circle of blackness closed gently over its brilliant and tragic center as if some one had softly closed the diaphragm of a camera. . . .

The next thing Socorro knew she heard her mother's excited voice crying, "Loosen her collar, Margherita—a little water there, Narciso—" then she became conscious that her face was wet.

Señor Montauban was saying, "She has worn herself out nursing Rafael; this excitement was too much for her."

Some one was chafing her hands and Margherita's voice was quavering, "Socorro, darling, do open your eyes! Can't you hear me? It's Margherita!"

When Socorro opened her eyes she found herself

stretched out on three seats in the box. With a
great effort she lifted her head and saw the black
mules dragging the dead bull out of the arena.
Applause broke out in other sections of the amphitheater. The herald blew a blast on his bugle to
proclaim the human victor in the fight. The band
burst into a mist of music.

The Señora Jiminez was saying that they must
go at once. Socorro hardly could realize that she
had fainted. She attempted to persuade the party
to remain through the *corrida*. She tried to get
her mother and Margherita to stay in the box and
let Señor Montauban take her home in his motor,
but they would not hear of it.

"This is a punishment for going off and leaving
Rafael!" declared the Señora, rather awed by the
swiftness of the divine disapproval. "I felt something was coming all the time."

"There will be a lot of gossip about this," wailed
Margherita, "this happening after that. I mean,
you know what I mean, our going as we did . . ."

She clattered away as she held one of Socorro's
arms and the little party made its way along the
aisle behind the boxes to the great castellated entrance of the *circo*.

Señor Montauban was on the other side of the

invalid. He made little explanatory speeches to his friends as he passed their boxes: "Overwrought from nursing her brother." "Unstrung from lack of sleep . . ."

There was something about the dapper little fellow which was distasteful to Socorro's shocked nerves. His stature, his arm about her waist. She was glad when they got to the motor and he loosed her. She took the priest's place in the back seat, leaning back in a corner with Margherita's arm about her shoulders. Señor Montauban occupied the front seat alone as he drove back to Paraiso.

Chapter 8

WHEN Señor Montauban delivered his unfortunate box party at the Jiminez home, Socorro Jiminez walked weakly up the long path from the tall iron fence to the house. She retired immediately to her bedchamber and lay down on a pink-covered bed where the maid, Lizetta, removed her slippers and loosened her dress, while Margherita helped make her friend comfortable with a sympathetic monologue.

"The excitement was too much for you, *carissima*. I am sure it was a judgment of Providence, for we really ought not to have gone out so soon after Rafael's illness. At least it was ill-mannered and one might as well be wicked as ill-mannered. If I were Providence I would punish one as quickly as the other."

Later Lizetta prepared the invalid a cup of strong coffee. The Señorita Jiminez drank the black liquid, then Margherita closed the jalousies to keep out the green glare reflected from the shrubbery, and the friend and the maid tiptoed from the room.

Socorro Jiminez remained in the cool semi-dark chamber with the vision of the bullfight still harassing her nerves. The fight was still in progress, she knew that. It would continue for some two hours longer. She lifted her head and tried to make out the time from a little gilt clock on her dressing table. She could see merely the round blur of its dial and this shook slightly to a throbbing in her eyes. For two more hours bull after bull would be turned into the arena, and if Angelito made any false step, any miscalculated movement, it might result in his sudden and terrible death. The very midriff of the girl seemed to writhe within her. Lying down became unbearable. She pushed herself up and stared about her chamber.

"Holy virgin," she murmured, "I think I must be mad! I have overworked from nursing Rafael." But the mere thought of Rafael reproduced the blue *casa* on Traposo *calle*, the queer ornamentation of his sick room, the tinted columns of the *patio*, and the owner of the *casa* whose eyes had followed her perpetually as she came and went. And now this man who had watched her so unhappily was fighting bulls in the *circo* at this very moment.

She drew a deep breath, then thought: "Nothing will happen to him. He has been our leading *diestro* for years. Nothing will happen to him . . . I wonder where he came from . . ."

She lay back down, closed her eyes and tried to drop off into a siesta, but she remained intensely awake behind her closed lids. She wondered where Angelito had come from and she thought of Señor Montauban and her approaching marriage to him. The idea of her marriage brought her a queer little feeling of distress. Heretofore the notion of marriage with the little editor connoted mainly the managing of the Montauban château, directing the Montauban servants, preparing for balls and dinners and driving in the Montauban motor. Narciso, heretofore, had entered into these reveries as a graceful partner. Now as Socorro lay with closed lids this strange internal commotion within her made her realize that marriage was something quite other than these things. That it was a vital and formidable thing; that out of the obscure clouds of marriage some sort of emotional and spiritual storm would surely beset her.

A vivid image of Señor Montauban popped before her eyes. His baldness, his witheredness, his precise articulation, all a little exaggerated, a little

burlesqued, as if some imp in her brain would cari-
cature him. As she stared at this image and
thought of his paternal criticisms, his meticulous-
ness, his disagreeable little gusts of caresses, a sort
of horror passed over Socorro.

She opened her eyes, got up abruptly from her
bed, thrust her small silk-clad feet into red boudoir
slippers and moved nervously about the room. As
she passed her mirror she paused to correct her
disheveled appearance; she fastened her dress at
the throat, tucked in a few loose strands of hair.
Then she opened the door of her room onto the
patio.

The glare of yellow sunshine made her blink for
a moment, then she walked across the *patio* to the
room opposite her own. The door of this chamber stood open and looking through the entrance
she saw Rafael leaning back among a pile of pillows with a writing board propped against an up-
raised knee. There was a look of suffering and
cynicism on her brother's handsome face which
Socorro had never observed before. As the girl
came through the sunshine to his room, Rafael
glanced up at her and continued gazing at her ab-
stractedly for several moments as if he did not
see her. Then he said, as if faintly startled, "Ah,

come in, Socorro; *Maman* and Margherita told me about your fainting at the *circo*. The sport seems to be rather hard on us Jiminezes." He smiled slightly. "How do you feel now?"

The girl entered the room and noticed its smell of cigarette smoke, "Better, *gracias;* the coffee helped me I think."

She hesitated a moment as Rafael motioned her to a chair, then as she sank into it she asked, "Did they tell you why I fainted?"

"They said you were worrying over me . . ." He paused a moment, regarding her interrogatively, then added, "I didn't exactly believe that."

"No?"

"No, but I didn't say anything."

"Why?"

Rafael made a weak discouraged gesture with his hands.

"I've quit talking to them, Socorro."

The girl was shocked. *"Anda,* Rafael, you don't mean it!"

"Yes I do—what's the use, they never understand what I'm talking about?"

"They understand Spanish, Rafael."

"You know what I mean. Everything I think or say is simply foolishness to them."

Socorro sat staring at her brother. "And yet you are going to marry Margherita!" she observed anxiously.

Rafael looked at her with a faint quirking of the lips.

"I believe I am not the only one in this *casa* about to be married . . ."

Socorro's face reddened somewhat and she looked away at the sharp definition of the sunshine where it fell in through the doorway. It was so bright that it seemed a white ethereal flame burning on the floor. After a while she asked, "What are you writing?"

"A poem."

"Read it to me."

"It isn't finished."

"What are you going to call it?"

"Glands."

Socorro looked once more at her brother with her first touch of interest in the topic.

"Glands—what a queer name for a poem!"

"*Cá*, yes it's queer! I call it that to be different. Everything I do or say, Socorro, you understand, is merely to be different!"

In the girl's tremulous mood this faint irony filled her with a profound pathos. She leaned forward impulsively and pressed the hand of the invalid. "Poor Rafael, I suppose you are quite alone writing your poems!" She gave a deep sigh and leaned back with arms outstretched so she might still hold the wounded man's hand. "I do wish Margherita could understand you a little better, Rafael, I do indeed!"

"Do you remember the Greek myth, Socorro, about Paris and his golden apple?"

"*Pues*, yes?"

"I am sure he would have liked very much to divide his golden apple between Venus and Minerva and have given each goddess half, but that was impossible. There is no way to divide the apple, Socorro, nor to combine the two goddesses into one. I think every human being reaches an impasse of this sort at last."

"What a terrible idea!"

"No, it simply means this: every person's idea of happiness is a bundle of contradictions. To acquire one thing, a person must sacrifice some other thing. The more you think about it the simpler it grows and . . . the more absurd."

Socorro was shocked at this unexpected revelation of her brother's chronic unhappiness. It appealed to her more keenly now that he was crippled. She felt tears wet her eyes as she gazed tenderly at him. "But surely, Rafael," she cried, disregarding the logic of his pessimism, "surely out of a whole city you can find some girl who will bring you sympathy and understanding and—and all your heart desires."

The poet stroked his sister's fingers with a mirthless smile. "That seems true to all persons when they are young and unphilosophic, Socorro. Every person feels that somewhere on earth is a perfect being who will understand him deeply and satisfy him profoundly, but—the wait stretches out and out and finally we grow weary and begin to lose faith in our ideal who never, never comes, and at last we marry just an ordinary person and that phase of life is finished and done."

Socorro leaned forward with horror on her face. An understanding born of her own new passion shook her.

"Oh, Rafael, don't say that! Don't think it, dear Rafael! You know God would not mock our dreams if they could never, never be realized."

She slipped an arm about his neck and began weeping softly on his shoulder, spending her pain of the *circo* in her grief.

The poet put an arm about his sister and stroked her shoulder. "Hush, Socorro; very likely I am all wrong. My thoughts wander about madly and contradict themselves. Sometimes I have thought that our first dream of love seeks no mortal at all, but that we are trying to unite ourselves with God. Our desires are so vague and mysterious and half religious. Dear sister, I don't know who has stirred you so that you faint at the *circo* and then come weeping to me, but I know it was not my wounds that did it. A sister's kindness is more composed than that."

Socorro felt her brother pat her face and press her hot cheek against his own. She lay breathing unevenly and was rather awestruck at the depth of her brother's wisdom.

"I don't know how to answer you," she said at last.

"Then don't answer me at all."

Came a silence, then she began tentatively, "At the *circo* I—I could not endure to see—" and she stopped.

"Yes, *carissima* . . . ?"

"To see the—the bull charge—"

"Yes?"

"Angelito," she whispered, and her face swept hot again.

Came a sudden silence.   Socorro felt her brother turn his head a trifle to glance down at her face. She turned her hot face away from his eyes, flooded with a sense of shame and wondering what he would say.

"Angelito!" repeated Rafael in an amazed voice.

She nodded faintly, all her senses painfully alert to catch his next reaction.

Came a long disheartening pause, then Rafael asked, "But, Socorro, how could you have known him at all—did you talk with him when I was sick?"

The girl shook her head mutely.

"Did he send you messages?"

"No."

"Then, Socorro, dear sister, how—what—"

The girl turned her face under her brother's chin.

"Oh, Rafael, I don't know—he just kept looking at me!   Margherita noticed it; everybody noticed it.   That was why *Maman* was so unpleasant to him.   And he seemed so strong and so unhappy. And his poor dinner!   He needed some girl so badly to keep things straight for him.   And now what

you say about every man waiting for some one . . .
it is pitiful . . . everybody is pitiful, and he seems
the most pitiful of all . . ."

Here Socorro clutched her brother's neck and began sobbing frankly out of pity.

Rafael held his sister silently and enigmatically.
At last she ceased weeping and asked in a small
voice, *"Pues,* what am I to do?"

"I—don't know."

"I don't suppose I shall ever see him again except when he is fighting bulls, and that makes me
faint."

"Angelito . . ." repeated Rafael.

Socorro moved her head a trifle. "Are you going to be against me too?"

"I?"

"Well, you know everybody is going to be against
me, *Maman* and Margherita, and—and everybody.
I'm going to have a terrible scene if this comes out."

Rafael drew a long breath that lifted Socorro's
head a trifle. "No-o-o," he dragged out at last, "I
am not exactly against you, Socorro."

"Then you'll talk for me against *Maman* and
Margherita?" she asked quickly. "You know,
darling, you talk so well."

Rafael was not prepared to argue that he didn't

talk well. He cleared his throat and said nothing.

"So I am going to expect you to, Rafael," said Socorro, sitting up and looking at her brother with a flushed face.

"*Pues*, you have philosophy on your side, Socorro, biology, an instinctive return to the earth. You know the old fable about the wrestler Anteus, who, each time he was thrown to earth, arose stronger than ever—well, the passion of the aristocrat for . . ."

Socorro did not follow her brother's application of the old fable of Anteus. Love and admiration for her brother flooded the girl. He was going to talk for her. She knew that he would so mix up ther and Margherita that neither could make heads or tails of what he would say. There would be much recrimination, but nevertheless it was far better that she should have Rafael on her side than against her. Nobody could be positive that what he said meant anything. And whether he meant anything or not he would talk endlessly and cuttingly, and she could sit silent through it all. She was delighted to get Rafael on her side. She pressed her cheek to his once more, then got up and went quickly to her room.

She hardly knew why she had done any of these

things. But her talk with Rafael apparently had started her on a course of action which she now pursued swiftly and mechanically. She went straight to her room and wrote a note. The note said:

To His Excellency, Señor Gabrielo Angel:
Estimable Señor, I think you are not treating my brother very kindly to save his life, take him into your *casa*, and then desert him without a word. We would be very glad to see you if you can find the time to call. We are at home any evening after seven. With the utmost respect, I am

Your *amiga*,
SOCORRO DE JESUS JIMINEZ.

As she placed this note in an envelope, she was wondering, with a certain discomfort, what Narciso Montauban would think about that.

Chapter 9

AFTER the trumpet had sounded the death of the last bull and the mules had trotted in and dragged out its body, the trumpeter, high up on the northern tier of seats, wiped the mouth of his instrument and slipped it into its dirty bag, then stood yawning and looking indolently about him. Already the spectators were trickling through the great oval incline of seats toward the exit. A thin applause still rattled over the amphitheater, but it hardly served to displace the essential stillness of the *circo*. The bullring possessed that wide stillness inherent in all huge structures and which the talk and movement of the thinly strewn spectators did little to dispel.

As the mules dragged out the last dead bull, the *banderilleros* and *espadas* went about the long circling balustrade gathering their cloaks which they had flung up at the beginning of the *corrida*. Those spectators who had been honored with a cloak still lingered in their boxes to toss back the garment and exchange a compliment with the fighter. Such trifling courtesies were going on all around the oval.

Angelito walked quickly toward the press box, looking forward to this slight social contact with Socorro Jiminez. When he reached the place he saw it was deserted; that his carmine cloak was spread on the balustrade of an empty box.

The bullfighter stood on the sand below looking up at the piece of carmine velvet left hanging on the rail. A devotee of the sport, three boxes distant, saw the *espāda's* plight. He came hurrying around to throw the cloak down to its owner. The man himself seemed incensed at such an indignity.

"*Caramba,* Señor Angelito," he cried, as he brushed away some speck of dust on the velvet, and then swung it carefully down into the hands of its owner, "you must excuse such boors. She was doubtless some pretty *mujer* from the provinces who understands nothing."

The *torero* did not know the man who tossed him his cloak. He bowed with a hot face, murmured a "*gracias*" and went hurrying away toward the dressing room at the southern end of the *circo*.

In the dressing room Angelito found some of his fellow players taking off their bright ring costumes while others were already in the showers washing

off the sweat and smell of the bullfight. No one
had been hurt and they were all in a gay mood,
shouting and laughing at each other amid the splash
and hiss of the water. Much of their talk was of
the coming Spanish *corrida* and of who would be
second *espada* to the great Juan Leon.

Ercolito, a mulatto with slim legs, large feet and
splendidly carved shoulders, shouted out that he
did not want the place. He said he was accustomed to standing up before the slow Creole bulls,
and the idea of facing a fast Spanish bull was
enough to make him . . . Here Ercolito used an
obscene comparison which set the dressing room
laughing. The other attendants and the youthful
monosabios began using the same gross jests, each
one attempting to speak a little more foully than
the last.

Of late such grossness had become detestable
to Angelito and at this moment it accented the insult he believed Socorro Jiminez had given him,
and somehow it seemed to justify that insult. She
was right in refusing him the small courtesy of
tossing back his cloak. All bullfighters were lewd
fellows. So he had been till he met her. They
were nothing but peons whom a turn of fortune had
thrust into the glare of fame and huge salaries, but

peons they were and peons they would remain, foul of mind and heart.

The *torero* finished dressing as quickly as he could and got away from his companions. He started back through the arena somberly enough, meaning to catch a 'bus in the plaza. By this time the amphitheater was entirely deserted. The declining sun filled it with a yellow light which blurred the distant sweep of seats into an ocherous slope. It might have been that yellow cloud, which Angelito so often imagined, that lowered Socorro Jiminez every Sunday afternoon in order that she might see him risk his life in the bullring for her amusement, and then, when he had finished, it lifted her back up into the heaven from whence she came.

That was a heaven forever closed to him. He could only stand on the solid sand, caked by the blood of bulls he had slain, and see her float away from him without so much as a word.

If she had given him only a moment's chance what would he not say to her! He would say, "Señorita, I know I am a vile fellow, but the very look of your heavenly face has purified my heart. Indeed, Señorita, you are like the saints in the cathedral, the mere thought of you saves me from all sinful fancies. Only that moment, Señorita, I was driven out of the dressing room because your image filled my heart, and I could not bear to hold your image in the presence of such obscenity. And yet you insult the poor cloak of the man who worships you!"

The *torero* made a tragic gesture as he hurried along in the immensity of the *circo*. He felt the high purity of his rôle with a Latin sense of drama.

As he passed out, he heard the ticket seller whistling gaily in his little booth in the outer wall. Angelito could see him behind the bars of the ticket window hurrying through the last of his accounts.

The *torero* hissed at a cab on the other side of the plaza and then stood looking at the ticket vender with a change of mood.

"Now listen to that ticket butcher whistle," he thought gloomily; "he is hurrying through to go to see some *querida*, some simple, or perhaps some questionable *mujer*, and here I stand, Angelito, the premier *espada* in Caracas, who makes as much in one Sunday afternoon as that *bribon* does all year long, and I feel as if ten devils were lodged in the pit of my stomach. *Diabolo!* I should say there are a hundred *señoritas* in Caracas who would welcome me to one who would glance at that *bobo*.

That shows what a fool I am to stand here thinking of a girl who leaves my cloak hanging on her
balustrade when I could go to a score of women!"

He hissed again at the cabman who, this time
caught his sibilance, pulled his horses around, and
trotted toward the *torero*.

As the cab came across the square, Angelito
turned over in his mind several addresses at which
he knew that he would be very welcome indeed.
He selected one. "All I will have to do," he mused
as the cab came up, "will simply be to step in, call
that address, and then sit still. That is all I will
have to do. . . ." But when the cab reached him
the thought of calling on any other woman was as
repugnant to the *torero* as had been the conversation in the dressing room. He stepped into the
vehicle, gave his own address on Traposo *calle* and
rode away. This struck Angelito as an extraordinary conclusion to his musings, also rather a dis-
tressful one.

"*Caramba*," he thought, "how long am I to be
deprived of all the natural pleasures of men just
because a *señorita* refused to toss back my cloak.
Certainly I am as mad as a crab that runs backwards from everything it sees."

In this predicament he leaned forward impulsively and shared his trouble with the driver, as one peon confides in another.

"Brother," he shouted earnestly above the rattle of the cobblestones, "a woman is a terrible thing!"

The cabman turned, looked down from his perch and took an immediate and intimate interest in his fare. "That is true, Señor," he agreed earnestly; "doesn't Pedro Ibana know that? A bad woman, Señor, is a limb of Satan. Everything goes: a man's money, his health, reputation, his peace of mind, *Cá*, Señor, his very soul! If there is a man in Caracas who knows that, Señor, it is Pedro Ibana!"

"Hombre!" cried Angelito, leaning forward and holding to the top as the cab jounced over the cobbles. "What you say is true enough; a bad woman is the whip of the devil, but if you want to roast on the very grid of hell, Señor Ibana, go to a good woman!"

Señor Ibana was amazed. He stared at his fare with his whip poised. "A good woman, Señor!"

"Sí, Señor, a good woman! She spoils all a man's natural enjoyments and furnishes none in return. You cannot leave her and forget her as you would an ordinary baggage, *Dios in cielo!* you cannot do that any more than you could turn away from the saints in Paradise. Ah, Señor Ibana, I

know of no sadder sight than to behold a man with all the simple pleasures of his life corrupted by a good woman!" Angelito made a hopeless gesture with his free hand and sank back against the cushions of his bumping cab.

The cab driver had been a comfort to Angelito, for the *torero* was of the temperament that must talk to some one when he was troubled. Now the cab stopped and delivered him to the emptiness of the blue *casa* on Traposo *calle* and he was alone again.

For several minutes the fighter stood at his doorway looking at the opalescence of the mountains in the last of the sunlight, but it was a mechanical gazing toward a brilliant view; he did not see it. He hated going inside. He hated seeing his mother, who, he knew, would begin reviling the Jiminez family again. Heretofore he had defended them, but Socorro's deliberate insult would stop his mouth; he could only sit silent and hear his vitriolic old mother scold and scold. He thought of the girl again, how she had reached out for his cloak, caught it eagerly, then had gone away and left it . . .

Angelito could not understand these two contradictory gestures. He did not attempt to understand them. Simply, they were. She had welcomed his cloak, then had deserted it.

The *diestro* drew out his keys, unlocked the bronze grating of his door, then the small inner panel, and let himself inside.

To Angelito, the whole interior of his *casa* was redolent of Socorro Jiminez. As he walked into the entry it seemed to him that he might meet her coming out. In the *patio* it seemed certain that presently she would come out of the front room and pass among the twisted pink columns. The ornate columns suggested the warm loveliness of the girl. They were two components of a whole and Angelito could never see the one member without recalling the other.

The bullfighter moved slowly down the *patio* past his dining room which had not been used since the evening of the banquet. He and his mother now ate their meals on a table in the kitchen because the dining room table was occupied by the big chest of silver. Old Ana had repacked the whole set, wrapping each piece in its original tissue paper, and now the chest awaited in a sort of indefinite suspense. Neither Angelito nor his mother quite knew whether it would eventually go back to the jeweler at a discount, or be sold to some other buyer, or whether it would remain in the blue *casa* as a nucleus of family plate to admonish other lives in years to come with the brave legend, "To the Stars through Difficulties."

As Angelito's footfalls sounded through the *patio*, a door opened farther down and old Ana hurried out of her room.

"*Gracias* to the saints, Pancho," she cried, "you are not hurt! I heard your footsteps coming so slow I thought you had been wounded. You gave me a turn, *mi hijo!*"

"No," said the *espada* briefly, "the *corrida* was dull, tame." He meant to stop with this information, but he could not help adding, "I saw the Jiminez family in the press box."

"You did! Is Señor Rafael able to be out so soon?"

"No, Rafael was not there."

The old peon woman appeared shocked. "*Cá!* These hard-hearted aristocrats! A mother and a sister go right off to a bullfight after their boy has been hurt in one, *Caramba!*"

"Ah, *madre*, they needed the air. They have been bound hand and foot with Rafael for a long time."

"They could have taken it a little more decently

than by going to a bullfight. I say it looks heartless." She paused in her carping to look sharply at her son. "I suppose you flung up your cloak to the Señorita Jiminez?"

"No, I didn't," denied Angelito, hoping to avoid a rehearsal of the whole event.

"You didn't! Well, I'm glad of it—who did you fling your cloak to?" Her astonishment admitted that the Jiminezes were the proper persons to receive this favor.

"To a—a stranger," hesitated the bullfighter.

But the way he said it told the old woman the truth. "Ah, *puf!*" she shrugged. "You are always lying to me, Pancho." She stood looking at him with reproachful eyes in her wrinkled old face, then added vindictively, "I wish you had not thrown your cloak to anybody. I wish you had just flung it down on the bench and let it lie there. *Caramba!* Those conceited Jiminezes!"

A hot flush swept over Angelito and he flung out impulsively, "*Diabolo*, so do I!"

The old woman stared. "So do you?"

"By the wounds of Christ!" shouted Angelito, "I do wish I had flung my cloak on the bench; I wish I had flung it in the dust!" He made a furious gesture.

His violence alarmed the old woman. "Holy Virgin!" she cried with distended eyes, *"Mi hijo,* what has happened?" She stepped quickly to him, caught his arm and peered anxiously into his face. *"Hijo mio,* what can have happened?"

The fighter's face darkened and his voice shook as he cried out: "A thousand devils, she flung it down! She flung it down in the ring there before all Caracas! She humbled me as if I had been a *monosabio,* as if I had been the very mule driver that hauls out the carrion!"

"Dios, have mercy!" gasped the crone, growing clay-colored at such an outrage.

"Such an insult was never borne before! God in heaven, if I were a peon, I would set their sugar field afire! I would hamstring their horses! God's lightning, I would poison their well!"

"Eh, eh, Pancho, my son!" warned the old woman fearfully. "Don't talk so loud! *Caramba,* suppose some one should hear you!" She glanced fearfully about the big empty *casa,* then for greater secrecy drew her son toward her own poor room.

"But in God's name," she asked in a shaken voice, "why did she do it? Have you not treated her with every respect?"

"She simply wanted to humble me, to show me

that I was nothing but a peon, that I was a mad
man to dream of looking at her. A thousand devils,
I am mad! I'm mad, mad, *madre!* I see nothing but that girl! This *patio,* my *casa,* the whole
city is filled with her. I never look anywhere but
what I see her just about to come to me. I think,
feel, hear, nothing but her, and she flings my cloak
in the dust!"

He was in his mother's room now with its earthen
floor and grass bed. He threw himself on the ancient mahogany frame face down with oaths and
sobs tearing at his throat.

The old woman stood aghast at this paroxysm
and gradually began weeping with anger herself.
She walked shakily to her crucifix hanging on the
wall with a candle beneath it. With trembling
fingers she struck a match and adjusted its flame
to the wick. The old woman knelt and lifted her
weeping, furious eyes to the image.

"O Cristo!" she quivered, "comfort me by de-
stroying these aristocrats! Bring death and deso-
lation to them! Pour your curses upon them. Let
the girl Socorro be a barren miserable woman, a
loveless bride and a childless wife! Thou know-
est the aristocrats did my husband to death, they
sent my brother to the 'reds,' they poured contempt

on me and now they despise my son! Curse them, San Pablo! Curse them, San Tomas! May their souls sink to . . ."

At this point in old Ana's malediction came a clangor at the doorbell.

Angelito sprang up from the straw mattress. *"Madre!"* he gasped, "hurry to the door! It must be the Señorita come to tell me she did not mean it! Hurry! *Pronto!"* he was lifting her from where she knelt.

As she was pulled up she cried out angrily, "Pancho, are you crazy?"

"Ana," said the bullfighter in a loud voice to his mother in his arms, "go to the door and see who it is."

The old woman shook herself free, looked sourly at her son, but went out and presently called back from the entry that it was a mulatto girl with a note.

The bullfighter was not accustomed to notes. He came out somewhat curiously into the *patio* and then recognized the Jiminez servant standing with his mother in the entry. Instantly he suspected that Socorro Jiminez really had sent him a note. It struck him that that would be what Socorro would do, write him a note, an apology perhaps.

His heart began to beat with a sudden happiness. The next moment he went hurrying toward the entry crying impatiently to his mother who stood looking blankly at the note. "Here, bring it here! Don't stand all day like that! What does it say?"

The servant girl turned to go.

"Hold on!" cried Angelito anxiously. "It may need an answer; *Diabolo,* some notes do! Wait a few minutes and I will see if it needs an answer . . ."

"My mistress said it didn't need an answer," said the girl, who still seemed on the verge of going.

"Your mistress!" echoed old Ana in surprise.

Angelito's heart gave a double beat. He was right. It was a note from Socorro. "Here, let me have it! Wait, *muchacha,* just a moment; let me read it!" He took the note from his mother and unfolded it with hurried fingers. A vague perfume arose. He read slowly, forming the words with his lips.

"To his excellency, Señor Gabrielo Angel. Estimable Señor, etc., etc. . . . we would all be very glad to see you if you can find time to call. We are at home every evening, etc., etc. Your *amiga,* Socorro de Jesus Jiminez."

When Angelito had read the note an amazing light-heartedness filled him. He felt like dancing, flinging his arms about the mulatto girl and waltzing in the entry.

"Tell your mistress I am coming to-night!" he cried gaily. "*Caramba*, to think she should write me a note! *Ola*, but it smells good!" He put it to his nose and inhaled, then kissed it.

"*Sí*, Señor," nodded the girl, beginning to laugh. "It smells like poetry."

"Oh, Señora, did you ever hear such a man!" cried the mulatto to Ana. "The *Señorita's* note smells like poetry!"

"He is mad!" declared old Ana ill-temperedly.

"Were you at the bullfight this afternoon?" asked Angelito with a desire to work off his ebullition by gossiping.

"*Sí*, Señor, I never miss a *circo* when you are in it."

"Is that true? You are flattering me. I only hope I will get into the big Spanish *corrida*."

"Oh, so do I, Señor!" cried the girl fervently. "I would much rather see you fight than Juan Leon."

"You will have your *chiste* (jest)!" exclaimed Angelito flattered. "*Pues*, tell your mistress I am coming down immediately, and I send her a thousand respects."

"I will, Señor, *adios pues.*"

"*Adios,* Señorita."

The girl went out into the street and the bull-fighter whirled and flung an arm about his mother.

"There you are!" he cried gaily. "A note from a *señorita.* Ah, *madre,* I told you I was a *caballero;* a peon would hardly get this from an aristocrat." He swung the note playfully under her nose.

"But you are not going, Pancho!" she cried indignantly.

"*Ciertamente,* I am going!"

"After she flung your cloak in the dust?"

The *torero* shrugged. "*Cá!* she didn't exactly throw my cloak down in the dust."

"You said she did."

"That was just a way of speaking. What she really did was to go off and leave it hanging on her box," the *espada* made a slight gesture, "that was all, just left it hanging on the rail of her box."

"*Diabolo,* that was all! Just left it hanging on the rail of her box! Wasn't that enough? Isn't it exactly the same as spitting on it? I am amazed at you, Pancho, to be ready to play the bear to a girl who has spit on your cloak, who has wounded your pride before all Caracas! Are you a dog or a man?"

"Now, *madre*," laughed Angelito, "if no man forgave his *querida* when she gave him the cold mutton, I'm thinking not many men and women would be on speaking terms."

"But *mi hijo!*" cried the old woman exasperated, "this was such a shameless insult!"

"*Cá!*" The fighter rolled his head complacently. "When a woman wants to attract a man's attention, *Madre*, she goes to extremes. It was her love . . ."

"*Huy! Huy!*" snapped the crone, completely out of temper. "What a fool! What a fool! Her love—it was her love! *Diabolo*, she is *sin verguenza!* A baggage who wants to show every one she can play fast and loose with the finest sword in Caracas—humble you to the dust one minute, toss you to the sky the next. Pancho, you would sicken a buzzard!"

"La! La!" interrupted the son with a good humor not to be dimmed. "I daresay you made my father dance to a pretty tune before he brought you around, eh, *madre?* Every *señorita* puts a man through his paces, doesn't she? I'll venture when you were a girl, you were driving men four-in-hand, now weren't you?"

The old woman blinked her eyes and grunted unintelligibly.

"I'll wager you were a regular devil among the boys. I always have thought it!" accused the *torero* in high spirits.

"I'm afraid," admitted the old woman at last, "I did nearly drive your poor father out of his wits, Pancho—and there were several other fine fellows, too . . ."

"I don't doubt it! I don't doubt it!" cried the *torero,* laughing loudly.

The old crone tipped her head to one side and her wrinkles took a humorous twist at the memory of some ancient caprice.

"Still, I never did write a note to a young man, asking him to come to see me, Pancho. I never did such a shameless thing in all my life."

The son ignored the fact that his mother never knew how to write. *"Madre,* a girl with a face like yours wouldn't have to write anybody, unless it was to ask the young men to leave her alone."

Old Ana cleared her throat. "Now, Pancho, you are laughing and trying to make sport, but—" she cleared her throat again, "that was exactly the way it was. . . ."

Chapter 10

IN a cab on his way to Paraiso, the bullfighter
drew out Socorro's note, touched it to his lips, inhaled its faint perfume and reread it in the last
light of day. It was unbelievable—a note from a
señorita in Paraiso! A note from the silent beautiful girl whose image still haunted his *casa*. And
now he was on his way to her villa at her request.

The fact that she had dishonored his cloak in the
circo only a few hours before now had no status
in his mind. Most persons can forgive wrongs, but
only lovers can forgive and utterly forget.

Angelito had his guitar with him in the cab. He
had brought it along when making a call as naturally as he took a rapier to the bullring. It was
his custom as a peon. Now the feel of it under
his hand, the rumor of music aroused in its belly
by the jolting of the cab, evoked in the *torero* a
mood of peculiar coloring which heightened his
sense of triumph. The faint sounds recalled his
Matadero days when he had used this same guitar
before the barred windows of *muchachas* in the

slaughter house slums. They were draggled, smelly purlieus. He had had to fight in these obscene streets with other peon youths for the right to stand at the girls' windows. He recalled how he and his rivals butted with their heads, kicked with their feet and knees and struck with the heels of their palms. He recalled one fight vividly. His rival danced about in the dust, feinting this way and that with his head and his feet, but he, Angelito, had leaped forward, his dirty head had crashed into the lad's belly and down he went; then he, Angelito, had kicked and stamped his prostrate foe. During this fight, the *muchacha* sat clutching the bars, peering out in silence.

Even now as he refought this battle in the solitude of his cab, his heavy muscles tensed and flexed to the remembered action.

In the midst of the conflict he drew a deep breath of thankfulness, *"Pues*, that was finished." Out of such obscene surroundings and feline courtships he had climbed to the decorum and amenities of Paraiso. He was a *caballero*. He would soon be in the presence of Socorro Jiminez. The thought sent a warm tingling through his whole body.

In the midst of this reverie his cab pulled up and Angelito discovered that they had reached the

tall iron fence of the Jiminez villa. He stepped
out with the nimbleness of his profession. He had
a feeling that he had ridden straight from his old
Matadero days into Paraiso. He paid his fare.
The driver turned his vehicle and drove off.

Angelito walked slowly toward the Jiminez gate,
holding his guitar by the neck. For the first time
a doubt assailed him as to the propriety of the instrument. He became unsure that guitars were
used by lovers in Paraiso. As he stood beside the
iron gate with its vertical bars reaching twice as
high as his head, he touched its strings dubiously
and evoked a queer melancholy chord in which
the peons cast their songs. It was neither major
nor minor, but a more melancholy sequence of intervals than either. Into this form had been
poured the sorrows of the Venezuelan peon whom,
for four hundred years, the Spanish had enslaved,
ravished and betrayed.

Angelito stood picking these chords and the
sound somewhat reassured him, for he opened the
gate and passed into the Jiminez grounds.

As he walked in with his strings whispering their
chords, the view of the shadowy villa set up another
question in his mind. The house was so large he
did not know at just what window he would find

Socorro. He did not even think of ringing the doorbell. He had always gone to the window of his *querida* with his guitar and that was what a call meant to him. But this villa held so many windows it seemed certain he could never find Socorro at all. Instinctively, he deserted the main path and moved diagonally across the lawn, scanning each window in its turn. In some of them the last umber of the west glimmered like miniature sunsets, others were already black with the coming darkness.

The shadowy lawn was sweet with evening fragrances and the air was full of those endless insect noises which compose the silence of a tropical night. As the bullfighter moved through the lawn, careful to make no noise, these insect voices became audible. It was a curiously complex orchestration, the thin montonous chirping of crickets, the sudden *arpeggio* of *cicadæ*, the bombilation of beetles, the dry shrill of some insect's tiny plectrum and the bird-like "ko-keet," "ko-keet" of the tropical frogs. Immediately in front of him over an acanthus bush, Angelito saw two great white moths dancing around and around each other in the purple air. As each one circled near him he could hear the furry whisper of its wings. Which pursued or which evaded in their tireless spiraling, he could not tell. For a moment he stood watching these airy lovers caught in the whirl of some unimaginable ecstasy. On a leaf of the acanthus glimmered a glowworm like some wise virgin with her tiny lamp, awaiting the coming of her groom.

Compared to the man on the lawn and the girl in the villa, these insect lovers were sundered by enormous distances, and their modes of courtship were infinitely tedious and complex; the glow of the worm, the circling of the moths, the clashing of plectra and the wail of tiny pipes. As Angelito moved about the villa amid this frail and passionate orchestra he heard the distant notes of a piano.

The sound sent a quiver of relief through the bullfighter's chest. He went quickly around the west wing of the villa and presently in one of the windows he saw a yellow glow. By moving around a flowering shrub he saw, through the bars, a girl seated at a piano with a floor lamp beside her.

The richness of the ensemble and the beauty of the girl struck Angelito like a strain of music. A hope that the girl would come to the window and talk to him seemed a sort of impossible happiness. He hardly knew Socorro; he had been accustomed to the severe apron in which she had nursed her brother. Now the white gleam of her arm through her slashed sleeve, her hair in shining black cables, her filmy décolleté gown, the sweet smooth line that curved from her chin to the dimple at the base of her throat all filled Angelito with a kind of despairing ecstasy. It seemed impossible that such a girl could be friendly toward him. She seemed too . . . expensive. She was so obviously reared to become the wife of some extensively wealthy man . . .

The bullfighter drew in his breath to call her, but the presumption of announcing himself to such a creature silenced him. He stood looking at her silently through the bars and presently became aware of the music she was making.

Socorro Jiminez was playing a piano transcription of Rimsky-Korsakov's Hymn to the Sun from The Golden Cockerel, but Angelito had not the faintest idea of its source, nor indeed had he ever heard its like before. He stood listening to the sad, wistful melody with its delicately repeated *cadenzas,* and it seemed to him as if it were the meditation of the girl herself, so pensive, exquisite and vaguely ironic.

Angelito stood listening with a beating heart and presently there formed in his mind a possible accompaniment to the delicately spun melody.

Looking fixedly at the girl, after the manner of a peon musician, he swung his guitar across his body and his left fingers set themselves to the frets, moving up and down the neck of the guitar, changing positions in silence with the sharp attack of a skilful guitarist. After some half a dozen changes in this mute accompaniment, Angelito caught the exotic motif of the Hymn, then, with his eyes fixed steadily on the softly lighted figure at the piano, he struck his strings and there arose a surprising harmony around the piano score.

At his first notes the girl at the instrument hesitated, but after a swift glance toward the window, she continued playing with the color mounting slowly to her face; then presently it faded again as she reëntered the spell of the great Russian.

The strange melody filled Angelito's head with a kind of swimming delight. His fingers flew over the frets following some instinct of their own. They wove ornaments and grace notes into the filigree of the music. With this accompaniment the girl at the piano passed swiftly into a new brilliance and passion of playing. The broken half-ironical pathos of Korsakov's melody, the little wistful questioning runs, the mournful solemnity of the bass, filled the salon and the darkening garden.

The pianiste played on and on to the last liquid double *cadenza* that cascaded from treble to bass, the last final queries following each other softly and hopelessly until the last question is left unfinished, its final note unsounded.

The belly of Angelito's guitar still vibrated under his fingers when he became aware that the girl had risen from the piano and was coming toward the window. She passed the lamp and became a lovely silhouette against its glow, and presently seated herself in the window so near Angelito that he caught the faint sweetness of her corsage.

She was saying, "That is you, Señor Angel, is it not?"

The bullfighter was so shaken that he could hardly answer, *"Si Señorita;* I received your compassionate note, Señorita."

"I did not know you played the guitar so beautifully; where did you ever get a guitar transcription of the Hymn?"

Her voice was so inviting and lovely that Angelito felt an impulse to kneel before her as he did to the saints in the cathedral.

"I never saw a transcription, Señorita—indeed, I know nothing about music; I play as I feel."

The girl peered at him attentively through the bars. "Señor, it is amazing—to follow such an intricate composition . . ."

Socorro's admiration loosed some of the endless soliloquies Angelito had spun about the girl.

"Señorita," he said intensely, "if I play at all acceptably, I owe it to you. Never before in all my life have I heard such mad sweetness as the air you played. It was like my thoughts of you, Señorita, a kind of honeyed aching, a grieving for some happiness that can never come in this life, at least not to so humble a man as I."

"*De verdad,* Señor!" exclaimed the girl. "I thought you were a *torero;* I did not know you were also a musician and a poet!"

"I am merely a man who reads a poem, Señorita. No man can look at you and not read a poem. If it did not come to his lips, it would rest in his heart."

"You are without shame," murmured the girl; "a sad flatterer and philanderer."

The bullfighter stood gripping the bronze grill with both hands. He could hear the blood in his ears. He could see the pale blur of her fingers around one of the window bars and instinctively he bent his lips to touch it.

"One does not flatter the moon by calling it lovely, Señorita, nor the sun by declaring it bright. Although you never spoke to me in my *casa*, Señorita, my heart danced to know you were there. When I played at dominoes in the cafés, I would suddenly think, 'I can go home and see her now.' It was like the sudden song of a bird."

Now, an American girl would have read into such hyperboles, and this kissing of fingers, the sure signals of insincerity, for in the high latitudes passion is dumb and its manifestations rough. But the Latin when aroused boils into dithyrambs and florid gestures. A Spanish-American girl is as deeply moved by the fevered eloquence and deferential kisses of her lover as a North American girl would be by the most dangerous choking and sputtering and the most painful blows, strange as that may seem to American readers. So Socorro Jiminez was not disgusted with the bullfighter's rhetoric as might reasonably be imagined; on the contrary, she was moved and began to explain why she had remained so silent and distant during her stay at the blue *casa*.

"It was because I misunderstood you, Señor,"

she said in an unsteady voice, "and I have been sorry for it ever since. I thought you were the principal cause of Rafael's going to Valencia and getting wounded. I did not know, Señor, I had no idea, that it was you who saved his life at the risk of your own. . . ."

"*Caramba!*" cried the bullfighter. "Think of all the lovely hours we wasted just because you did not know that one little thing!"

His regret was so naïve that Socorro broke out laughing and reached a hand through the bars to pat his arm. "Anyway, we know it now, and the world is not ended yet."

The bullfighter caught and kissed her hand again; the faint perfume of it set him trembling, but this second kiss ended this part of the interview rather abruptly, for she withdrew her hand and said, "Now you must go in and see Rafael; I know you are wanting to see him," and she arose from the window seat.

The bullfighter was as loathe to see Rafael at that moment as he would have been a devil out of hell. From head to foot he vibrated like a harp string. He listened as Socorro directed him around to a side door where she would admit him, then she left the music room. The night seemed to swing softly above Angelito. A quarter moon was in the sky, lodged apparently among the dark branches of a mamone tree. In its glimmer the white moths still whirled in their dance above the acanthus bush.

It seemed to Angelito the glamor of the night somehow cut him off from Socorro. The very moonlight was a sort of pale impalpable wall barring him from her. Amid this moving prison he walked to the side door. He knew that in just a few moments he would be inside talking to Rafael, and also, no doubt, to the coldly polite Señora. And so Socorro would be lost to him in the vacuity of formal conversation.

Rather unexpectedly, the door opened and the girl stepped out beside him for an instant. She paused to draw a breath of the perfume. "It's a sweet night, Señor."

Angelito sought to delay her. "You have so many flowers here, Señorita; it is like the fields of flowers the peons grow up in the mountains."

"Yes, I have seen them; they are very beautiful."

"And they grow the rarest varieties," wandered on the bullfighter, hardly observing what he said, "lilies and orchids . . ."

"If you are interested in orchids," exclaimed

Socorro impulsively, "we have a very rare one right out there in the garden, Señor Angel. It is one Rafael found up in the Goajiro country. It is pale blue and is fragrant only at night."

The implication that she was about to show him an orchid in the garden flowed through the *torero* with a sensation as of warm wine being poured in his veins. He said in a voice not steady that he wished above all things to see the orchid; she took his arm and together they turned out into the moonlight.

The extreme unconventionality of such a walk seized and shook Angelito. At every step he trembled lest the girl turn and go back. Then, as she went on, he began to realize that she was as deeply moved as he himself. This seemed impossible. That a *señorita* so finished, so exquisite, could be stirred by him! He heard her give a little intake of breath.

"What is it, Señorita?" he trembled, terrified lest repentance had set in.

She gave a little nervous laugh. "Señor, your arm might be a bronze arm off a statue." He felt the faint pressure of her fingers on his biceps.

"That came from fighting, Señorita," he said huskily.

"You must be terribly strong!"

The bullfighter made a deprecatory movement of his hand which caused his arm to swell and relapse under her fingertips.

After a little pause she said, "You made me very happy this afternoon, Señor, throwing your cloak to me in the arena."

A reminiscent pain arose in the bullfighter's heart. "I thought I would find you there when I came back after it, Señorita."

The girl gave a gasp and looked at him, her eyes two dark spots in the moonlight. "Oh, I did go off and leave it on the balustrade!"

Angelito made a gesture. "It was nothing, Señorita."

"But it *was* something, it was indeed! Did you get it back?"

The *torero* tried to dismiss the topic. "A man threw it to me."

"A man—what must the man have thought."

"I don't know, Señorita; nothing, perhaps. It was such a trifle."

The girl pressed his arm to accent her point. "But it was not a trifle; it was rude. I—we—we had some trouble in our box, Señor, a little accident, that's why I did it."

"Did it happen to you?" asked the *torero* in the exaggerated alarm of lovers.

"*Pues*—yes."

"What could it have been."

The girl hesitated. "Just a trifle, I—I grew ill —I'm afraid I fainted."

For some reason Angelito's heart began beating at this confession. Her weakness appealed to his immense strength. Impulsively he put his hand on her arm as if to give her some kind of retroactive support.

"But how came you to faint, Señorita?" he asked anxiously. "Were you ill?"

This man's distress over her moved Socorro in the most intimate fashion. She had not meant to tell him why she fainted, and yet it became utterly impossible not to. His hand on her arm seemed to be softly melting something within her. "I—I hardly know, Señor," she hesitated. "I saw you standing alone in the arena. I—I thought how Rafael had been gored . . . somehow I fainted . . ."

"Oh . . . on account of Rafael."

Socorro wanted to let that go, but it seemed to her as if she were practising on him some monstrous deception. Her bosom lifted and fell. She was trembling all over.

"No-o, Señor," she whispered, "I was afraid you would be gored."

"Me?"

She nodded mutely. She seemed about to fall.

"You fainted on my account!"

"Oh, yes . . . yes," she breathed, letting herself go into his groping arms, resting her devastating weakness on his powerful muscles. Her senses were in confusion. She resisted instinctively his hand under her chin to turn her face to his.

"No, don't—don't do that," she gasped, supported mainly by his arms and against his body. She did not know why she wanted to delay or refuse his kiss.

Angelito held her as carefully as if a priest had entrusted him with the holy chrysm. She was slighter than he had thought and was amazingly soft. He had never before placed a hand on a girl bred and reared for the express purpose of becoming a wife to a wealthy man. The peon women, of whom he had known enough, were all tough and rubbery. Socorro was as surprising as his first draught of absinthe. He wanted to pick her up bodily, to press her against his breast, but he was exceedingly careful of her and a little afraid he might somehow hurt her delicateness.

There was a stone bench near them and they got to it. As he sat holding her, it was all a blank mystery to him. He could not understand her amazing capitulation. She was obviously a *señorita*, a guarded and perfectly innocent girl. He did not understand the persuasiveness of his weeks of mute wooing in his own *casa*, the pathos of his unfortunate dinner, the romantic force of the dangers he met in the arena.

After an uncertain interval they began whispering about the last subject which had engaged their thoughts, Socorro's fainting at the *circo*. She had never done such a thing before. She supposed this must be love, it was not what she had expected. What did she expect? She hardly knew, something different, in some way. . . . As she murmured these things her head rested on his chest and she could hear his heart whispering in her ear. Her eyes fixed themselves on the crescent moon hung in the mamone tree. It seemed as if all of her cares and suspense and weariness had been drawn out of her mind and body forever. She had never experienced so profound a rest.

Presently Angelito leaned down and kissed her, but it scarcely rippled her crystalline mood. His caress seemed so normal.

Socorro had a curious impression that somehow the man and the night had changed places. It seemed at first that Angelito was her lover and the night a sweet and ambient setting. Now Angelito's arms and body were the setting which enabled Socorro to see for the first time in her life how sweet and beautiful was the tropical night. Heretofore the beauty of the night filled her with a sort of wistful sweetness; now its light and perfume showered upon her in a fulfilled sweetness. For this hour she and Angelito and the ancient Night existed.

The girl felt the bullfighter move and then lift her gently to one side. A sharp sense of alarm went through her. Then she became aware of two figures standing within a few yards of the bench.

She gave a little gasp as she stared at the two dark figures. She stopped a scream in her throat. She had a convulsive impulse to run. One of the figures was her brother, the smaller was Señor

Montauban. She had a sensation as if she were sinking through space. She fell and fell and fell. The two figures sank with her. She felt hot, then intensely cold.

She saw Angelito get up and advance toward the two men. Something in his walk gave her a terrible fear that he would attack them, perhaps kill them. She heard Rafael's voice, amazed and bewildered.

"Socorro, sister—is that you!"

Señor Montauban immediately interrupted in a strained tone, "A lovely night, Señorita."

Socorro made an effort to speak and heard a strange voice saying for her, "I brought Señor Angel out here to see that blue orchid. . . ."

Angelito, from his experience in Matadero courtships, was expecting every moment a personal assault from the editor; now he began to perceive none was forthcoming. He wondered if it were possible that the two men had not seen him sitting with Socorro in his arms, but their voices denied this merciful possibility. He turned to Socorro and included the whole company: "Shall we go in the house, Señorita? I wish to pay my respects to the Señora."

But no sooner had he mentioned the Señora than

he realized that, of all persons, he dreaded meeting her the worst.

"I am sorry I can't go with you," said the editor in his strained manner; "I was just going. I will say good night." He bowed and all three persons repeated his good night in unnatural voices. The editor turned toward the gate and was lost in the veil of moonlight.

As Rafael turned once more toward the house he said in his strange voice, "Narciso and I were growing uneasy about you, Socorro. We heard you go out into the garden some time ago. It was getting late."

Angelito was growing more terrified every moment at the prospect of meeting the Señora. He seized on this as an excuse. "Perhaps I'd better wait till later to see the Señora?"

Socorro gripped his arm. "Don't leave me!" she whispered desperately, but the very next moment, "Yes, yes. *Madre de Dios*, go at once!"

Rafael, who had started into the side door, now turned back at Angelito's suggestion. "No, come on in, Señor," he insisted with a certain determination in his tone. "My mother will want to see you and no doubt you will want to say something concerning my sister."

Socorro gasped, "Oh, Rafael!" and suddenly dropped the *torero's* arm.

Angelito felt as if unknown depths were opening beneath his feet. "Your sister," he repeated vacantly, and dimly realized that he would have to make a declaration to the mother, asking for Socorro in marriage. Rafael stood holding the door open for the two to enter.

As Angelito walked toward the drawing room, he realized the futility of possessing such muscles as his amid polite society. It profited him nothing to be able to toss Rafael out in the garden and to bind the women with one hand. It had even been out of the question to assault Señor Montauban in the garden, although the idea did pass through his head.

Rafael limped slowly through a corridor and across a *patio* to a lighted room. Angelito and Socorro followed. There was nothing whatever the bullfighter could do to soften or forestall the coming interview.

Rafael opened a door and stood aside to admit his two companions, not to say prisoners, into a large room filled with a rose-colored light. The Señora Jiminez was at a table placidly weaving lace on a pillow stuck full of pins. On the other side

Margherita Miraflores crocheted so rapidly that her needle was a blur of flashes.

At the entrance of the party both the ladies looked up, and at the sight of Angelito they stopped work in surprise.

"It's Señor Angel!" cried Margherita jumping up. "How kind of you to come to see us!"

The Señora was cooler. "Won't you have a seat, Señor Angel?" she invited, staring at him in amazement.

Rafael cleared his throat. "Angelito—I mean Señor Angel desires to present his respects to you, *Maman*," said the young man of the house with preternatural seriousness, "and he would like to speak to you concerning Socorro."

The Señora's surprise grew into amazement. "Socorro! He—he would like to speak about Socorro! What is there he can say about Socorro?"

"*Pues*, there are not a great many topics on which a young man can speak to a mother about her daughter," returned Rafael drily.

The Señora looked about the group. "Rafael— are you insane! Socorro, what is your brother saying—" For the first time she looked at Socorro, and now the girl's face frightened her. "*Mi hija*," she cried, "are you ill? How white you look!

What does this mean, Señor Angelito, what can it possibly be that you want to say to me?"

Angelito moistened his lips and stammered, "I— I want to ask your permission to—to pay my addresses to your daughter."

"Your addresses! Addresses! A bullfighter pay his addresses to my daughter!"—she had grown as pale as the girl now—"Señor, I do not want to appear rude under my own roof, but you must realize this is—effrontery—it is—"

"*Madre,*" interposed Rafael quickly, "I must tell you that Socorro has already dismissed Narciso's suit in favor of Señor Angel!"

"Socorro! Am I going demented! You dismissed Narciso—Narciso Montauban!"

"Only five minutes ago, *madre,* Narciso and I found them seated in the garden together, on the stone bench."

"Alone!"

Rafael made a gesture.

"*Dios in cielo!*" gasped the matron. "Has Socorro disgraced herself—at her age!" She turned furiously on the bullfighter. "You serpent! You intriguing peon butcher! Leave my house! Go! Never let me see your hulking form . . ."

She gave Angelito the impression that she was

about to annihilate him through mere spiritual wrath.

Margherita stared at her friend, gasping vacantly, "Socorro! No! This is impossible!"

Rafael made an harassed gesture, *"Caramba!* Don't be gasping and insulting every one like that, *Maman!* This is a condition to be faced, not something to exclaim over. I tell you Narciso Montauban has gone."

From Margherita: "Socorro! To throw over the whole Montauban estate!"

"The question is," pressed Rafael in polite exasperation, "shall we accept Señor Angel in Narciso's stead? At present, no one knows of Socorro's indiscretion in the garden except Narciso and Angelito and us . . ."

"Por l'amor de Cristo, Rafael!" cried the Señora. "Don't be calling him Señor Angelito, call him his proper name, Señor Angel."

"Señor Angel—his name is not Señor Angel!"

"In the name of heaven, what is it then? Narciso said it was."

"I—don't know," said Rafael blankly.

"What is it, *hombre?*" she demanded, turning fiercely on the fighter. "What is your name?"

Her attack was so abrupt the *torero* had a dazzled

sensation as if some one had struck him in the face. He was forced to answer immediately without a moment's forecast of the consequences.

"I am Pancho Pachecho, Señora," he stammered hurriedly.

"Pancho Pachecho!"

"*Sí*, Señora," he answered in an apprehensive tone.

"Pancho Pachecho!" Suddenly she began to laugh. "A Jiminez marrying a Pachecho!" She broke into a rage of laughter. *"Mi hija!* Do you hear that! A *bribon* named Pancho Pachecho is asking me for your hand!"

"Caramba! That's nothing to have hysterics over, *madre!"* cried Rafael. "I could have told you it was something like that! The man naturally has a name!" He turned to Angelito, "Señor Pachecho, you see my mother is over-wrought. I will call at your *casa* in the morning with her answer to your request. So until then I wish you *adios.*" He bowed as gracefully as his lame leg would permit. Angelito returned the courtesy, then, glancing anxiously at Socorro, "Señora, Señoritas, good night."

Socorro's lips made a movement of good night in her perfectly white face. A thought came to

Angelito that he was now seeing his last of Socorro. With all his strength and suppleness there
was no way in which he could brush this angry
family away and take her. They had him bound
and trussed with the invisible thongs of custom,
they raked him with social preëminence. His huge
strength was no match for them at all. As he
crossed the *patio* and went out of the side entrance
he realized that he had lost her.

When her lover had well departed, Socorro
walked over to a sofa, sat down on it and said,
"Now—begin."

"Socorro, what can you see in that hulking creature! A bullfighter, a peon tossed up by the
circo! How could you, how could we have the
effrontery to announce such an engagement to our
friends here in Caracas!"

"But, *maman*," interposed Rafael, "that is not
the question now. Socorro was sitting in the garden with him alone, at midnight!"

Margherita interrupted. "But, Rafael, no one
knows it but us and Narciso!"

"Doesn't that villainous bullfighter know it!"
cried the Señora. "Do you imagine he will fail to
spread news of his conquest in the wineshops!"

"Oh, *madre!*" cried Socorro, with a sick face.

"He will, of course he will!" insisted the Señora, amazed at her daughter's belief in her lover. "Socorro, you don't know such creatures. They don't understand—they simply do not understand the code of aristocrats. I don't doubt this moment he is telling some brother peon of sitting in a garden with a *señorita*—is that all you did, just sit?" She turned to her son quickly. "Was that all she did, Rafael?"

"Oh, *maman*, you were a girl once, you know about how a girl in love acts."

"Socorro!" cried the distracted mother. "How could you be so shameless? You are as bad as the American *señoritas* who permit—anything!"

"Socorro, you might at least have stayed behind your bars," reproached Margherita in a tone that suggested that much could be accomplished even behind bars.

"Yes," declared Rafael in a dry voice, "you might have stayed behind bars, Socorro. Innocence is a technical matter and should be observed like fish on Friday."

The Señora Jiminez looked at her son. "Rafael, I hope you don't mean you are condoning your sister's conduct!"

"*Cá!* It has its other side, *maman*—everything has its other side."

"Other side! What other sides are there but shamelessness, disgracefulness and scandal—there'll be oceans of gossip about this, Socorro, you may rest sure of that!"

Socorro made no reply to this, but sat looking anxiously at her brother.

Rafael hesitated at thus being appealed to. He possibly might not have entered the lists at all had not Socorro spoken for his patronage. So he cleared his throat and said, "After all, *Maman,* Socorro has a certain—well, a certain justification when one comes really to look at it."

The mother turned her attention to Rafael. "A certain justification!" she repeated, amazed.

"Yes, her action shows, I think I may say, a certain return to fundamentals . . ."

Margherita also stared at him. "Rafael, whatever are you talking about!"

"I am talking about Socorro and Señor Angelito. To me their sudden and passionate attraction for each other has something fundamentally healthful, and I may even say, beautiful, in it."

"Rafael," frowned his mother, "you surely are not going to fling out any ill-timed philosophy when your sister's honor is in question and your family is in trouble. This is no time for philosophy."

The young man hesitated when Margherita cried out, "Let him go on, just to see what he will say!"

Came a little hesitation and Rafael again caught Socorro's eye.

"It's just this," began Rafael, self-consciously, since his remarks were clearly to be taken as an exhibition of fantastic nonsense. "It's just this, I wanted to say—er—that all aristocracies are eventually refined away to impotence." He collected what he had thought on the subject by main force of memory. "They breed along one strain, aristocracies do, I mean, until that strain becomes so exaggerated it can no longer withstand the shocks of existence. An aristocracy, such as ours, gets overcerebrated, too much nerves, too little brawn; too much convention, not enough impulse. This—er—this affair of Socorro's is her natural impulse to return to brawn, and to follow impulse. Her children will be—er—stronger, in better equilibrium for it, and I honor her for it."

Margherita and the Señora listened to this salmagundi of big words without any patience at all.

"You mean you honor Socorro for dishonoring herself?"

"I think, *maman*, when her love impulse is strong enough to make her overstep our conventions it is a very hopeful sign," returned the poet bruskly.

"Why, that's absurd and irreverent!" cried the mother. "You make a virtue of wrongdoing!"

"Wrong!" Wrong!" cried Rafael. "Wrong is what reduces one's chances of perpetuating oneself, and right is what forwards those ends. Now, in this instance . . ."

"*Rafael!*" cried his mother. "I am ashamed of you, talking such nonsense and wickedness in this hour of trouble!"

"*Cá!* There is really no use discussing it. Let's drop it. The only point is, what is the best thing to do under the circumstances? Socorro was seen sitting in the garden with Angelito. All there is left for us to do is to accept the fellow and have the banns published."

Señora Jiminez suddenly began weeping. "Sacred Virgin, that is the only sensible thing you have said, but that is too true. Socorro has disgraced herself. She will have to say many a prayer for this! To have my family disgraced by such a marriage!" The Señora sat down by the table, sobbing helplessly, and dabbed at her eyes with her handkerchief.

Margherita went over to her future mother-in-law, took her hands, occasionally sniffing back her own sobs.

"M-Margherita," gasped the Señora, "I don't suppose you will w-want to enter a disgraced family, es-especially when y-your future husband holds such w-wicked and i-irreligious views . . ."

"Oh, th-they aren't Rafael's v-views," sobbed Margherita; "h-he d-doesn't bub-believe what he says. I-I don't think he-he knows what he believes . . ." and here she joined her mother-in-law in sobbing outright.

"Th-That is very charitable, Margherita," murmured the Señora, pressing her future daughter-in-law's hands.

Rafael heard himself classified as a moron and forgiven by Margherita. He shrugged faintly and glanced at his sister. Socorro's expression seemed disappointed. He shrugged again privately, to himself. Finally he said, *"Pues,* what shall I tell this Señor Pachecho to-morrow—that it's all right?"

"If you do," choked the Señora, "it will be on your own responsibility as the head of this house. I will have nothing whatever to do with it."

This, of course, meant that the Señora was giving her consent. The poet limped to his mother's side and patted her cheek. "After all, *maman*," he said gently, "this won't work out so badly. If you and Margherita could see this matter from my point of view it might make you more comfortable."

Margherita reached up and let her hands drag down his arms as he drew away from them.

"Good night, Rafael," she said wistfully.

"Good night," returned the poet. Then as he went out of the door into the *patio* toward his own room, he heard his mother begin again:

"Socorro, I simply cannot see what you find in such a creature. Why, he doesn't look like a man; he looks like a sort of bull . . . as if he had taken his figure from the animals he butchers."

Chapter 11

Rafael's dissertation on the right and wrong of marriage did not convince even Socorro Jiminez, but it did soothe and comfort the girl and lend her a certain moral support to know that her brother upheld her course.

Still, there was no escaping the fact that it was very, very wrong of her to sit in the garden with Señor Angel and allow him, nay virtually invite him, to kiss and embrace her as she had done.

After she had returned to her room that night, the enormity of her conduct so grew upon her and shamed her that she could not even remember how Rafael had arranged the logical members of his syllogism to make her appear in the right. Finally restlessness routed her out of her chamber and sent her over to Rafael's study for a restatement of the grounds of her defense.

But Rafael had that mercuric type of mind which never repeats a formula. This time he justified his sister's conduct by telling her that all human life was a compromise between the laws of society and the individual will. The objects of these two forces were usually diametrically opposed. Any social body made an effort to preserve itself, and that was the reason for the conventions against marriage outside of one's own circle. On the other hand, the individual was impelled toward misalliances to reinvigorate the original human stock with the increased vitality of a mixed breed. So all human life whirled about these cross currents; aristocracies tending to destroy life and preserve social forms; the individual tending to renew life and destroy social forms. "Now, that is why an outside marriage pleases a girl and shocks her family," smiled the poet.

"But which is right and which is wrong?" demanded Socorro with the feminine desire for a rule of thumb.

"My dear sister," laughed Rafael, "if you want a commandment, go to the priests; if you want to do as you please, come to the philosophers."

That was all she could get out of Rafael; nothing very definite or satisfactory. However, the Señorita was not really unhappy. Inside of every woman run two concurrent codes, and her fealty shifts from one to the other with the exigencies of her life. Socorro made her brother promise to go and tell Angelito the family's decision early next morning. Then Rafael kissed her, wished her, rather tamely, any happiness her proposed marriage might bring her, and sent her away to her own room while he resumed the grave task of putting into Spanish verse his thoughts on "glands."

Whatever was the disturbance in the Jiminez family, Angelito's pain was more acute than Socorro's because his sense of loss was more fundamental. It seemed to him that he had lost Socorro. He went to sleep with this hag riding his heart. At intervals, all night long, he would struggle out of the vague and symbolic torments of his dreams into a grey semi-waking hopelessness of ever possessing Socorro Jiminez. In his lethargic state, desire and tenderness flooded him. His memory became an inquisitor which tortured him with endless repetitions of the kisses he had received in the garden, of the softness of her flesh, of her arms about his neck, of the faint fragrances of her hair and body. And these graces, refinements, perfumes, voluptuousness were in conjunction with the sweetest and simplest innocence. It blended in him a fever of desire and a surpassing tenderness; the unstable combination of a lover. Her phantom

came and lingered beside him with an aching
sweetness.

Amid the pain of his erethism and hopelessness,
the music of the Hymn of the Sun slowly reëstab-
lished itself in his sleep-drugged brain, that strange
melancholy movement, the repeated, delicately
modulated *cadenzas*, which were like sad questions
asking: "Can this be Love? Is this endless grieving passion? O Night, does your sea-blue bowl hold
only the waters of desire and sadness and despair?"

The music throbbed in the bullfighter's brain. By
slow degrees his thoughts became bent and dis-
torted with returning sleep, and presently his brain
was filled once more with the jacquerie of dreams.

When Angelito arose at eight o'clock next morning, the braying of donkeys in Traposo *calle*, the
cries of the street venders, the sound of his mother
rattling pots in the kitchen tempered somewhat his
nocturnal impression that all existence centered in
and ended with Socorro Jiminez. The bustling,
matter-of-fact sounds suggested a certain possibility
of life proceeding without her. His bath helped
him. Amid a shower bath muscles become an end
in themselves. The sunshine slanting among the
pink columns of his *patio* suggested peace if not joy.
The black coffee his mother served him at the break-

fast table revived in him even a faint hope that his suit had not been utterly rejected. Rafael had promised to come and tell him the family's decision. However, if the decision were adverse, he did not expect Rafael to come. Among the Latins all couriers bring good news—or they bring no news at all. Almost unconsciously Angelito began listening for the doorbell. If the doorbell should ring—if Rafael should come—

As he sat sipping his coffee with rather a drugged feeling from his unwholesome night, there really did come a clanging at his door.

The bullfighter upset his coffee. A shock went through every nerve in his body. Old Ana, who had been smoldering at her son ever since he entered the kitchen, now burst into eruption. *"Caramba!* Look at you! Jumping like that was your passing bell! I knew you were waiting for somebody or something, a woman, a baggage, some *señorita* who doesn't care two centésimos for you and is after your bolivars!"

"Diantre!" cried Rafael. "Go to the door and see who it is! Don't stand there sputtering all day!" The bullfighter had half risen, but controlled himself and sat down again. The ring of the bell could mean only that Rafael had come with

an affirmative answer. He tried to take some coffee from his shaking cup into his dry mouth.

"Go on—don't stand there all day!"

Old Ana turned and shuffled off through the *patio* with an obstinate plopping of her *alpargatas*. Angelito watched intently as she disappeared among the columns. After a prolonged wait she reappeared, but this time wearing a sardonic smile in the wrinkles of her old weather-worn face.

Angelito watched her anxiously, wondering whom she had seen and what she had done. He thought with trepidation it was not one whit beyond her to refuse Rafael admittance to the house, or tell him that he, Angelito, was not at home. She might do anything.

She came plopping back with her enigmatic grimace, and then, when she was quite close to him, she drew from behind her a damp copy of a newspaper and flung it down on the table in front of him.

"There's your '*Sol y Sombrā*,'" she snapped. "That's what you were spilling your coffee and kicking the table over about! The boy had brought your '*Sol y Sombra*'!" Her sardonic smile grew sourer and she turned with a shrug to her pots again.

Angelito felt a peculiar tightening in his chest that comes of a sharp disappointment. He made an effort to hide this from his mother. He took up the paper mechanically and unfolded its limp pages. Over the front page was spread a long description of Juan Leon's fighting bulls and the complicated means by which these bulls were prevented from seeing a human being from the day they were calved until the moment they charged into the arena with barbs sticking in their shoulders.

Angelito could not read the article. The desolating fact that the Jiminez family had decided against him made reading impossible. He stared at the page and his eyes picked out isolated phrases: "raised on the loneliest *haciendas* . . . driven by night to railroad . . . shipped to the arena in closed cars . . . driven blindfolded to the *circo* . . . imagine the fury of a thoroughbred fighting bull when confronted for the first time in his life, in the glare and uproar of the arena, by his natural enemy, Man!"

Angelito's brain functioned sufficiently for him to know that he was reading about the coming Spanish *corrida,* and he began planning some sort of reprisal for his treatment by the Jiminez family.

In the coming *corrida* he would be second *espada*.
He determined when that moment came that he
would carry his part through with such spectacular
daring that Spanish impresarios would invite him
to the *circos* of old Spain; that eventually he would
be making a world tour with a shipload of fighting
bulls. And then when the Jiminez family saw they
had rejected a world-famous man, *Cá!* He could
imagine their sensations!

But then he thought that might make Socorro
unhappy, and he did not want to do that. The
very suggestion of Socorro filled Angelito with a
melting tenderness. He would never be allowed to
marry her, but even so he would always love her. In
the bullfighter's heart there grew up a dim prescience
of a tenderness and a love for a woman which
could persist quite without marriage or any physical contact. As he sat thinking on this new and
wistful possibility, he recalled tales he had heard
the priests tell of saints in old times who loved with
all the ardor and passion of earthly lovers, and yet
were monks. That was a strange thing, love di-
vorced from flesh, yet here in his own heart he
felt, reiterated, its possibility.

He sat thinking wistfully on this point when he
heard his name called from the *patio*.

The bullfighter looked around, straightened, then stared. Rafael Jiminez stood smiling at him in the *patio* at the entrance of the kitchen. Such a sudden flood of happiness swept over Angelito he could hardly find his voice.

"Rafael! It's you!" he cried in an amazed voice. "Does it mean I am fortunate? *San Pablo, hombre,* don't stand there laughing like that!"

Rafael spread his hands. "How do I know whether you are fortunate or not. You are accepted. That's not the same thing. Send old Ana off on an errand, *mi amigo,* and we will have a talk."

Angelito glanced at his mother uncertainly, and delayed action a trifle by asking Rafael how he got into the *casa*.

"I found the door unlocked. I thought, everything considered, I might walk in unannounced."

The bullfighter was more delighted than ever at this brotherly approach in Rafael.

"Sit down, here by the table," he invited rapturously. He turned to his mother again with some of his rapture vanishing.

"Ana," he hesitated, "you might go to the market now and buy our *comida*."

"Yes," interposed Rafael, drawing a coin from his pocket at the obstinate set of the old woman's face, "and take this, Ana; buy one of your lottery tickets and keep it for yourself. You might draw a fortune." He handed a five-bolivar piece to the crone.

The old woman took the silver sulkily, started off muttering, then suddenly broke into the violent obscenity of a peon enraged, and flung it on the tiles.

"Ana!" cried the bullfighter furiously, fearing this outburst would break off his delicate negotiations with Rafael.

Old Ana went on and the two men looked after her.

"Servants get like that when you keep them too long," observed Rafael; "they get to owning you. I shouldn't be surprised, when Socorro comes here, you would better get rid of the old *virago* and hire another girl."

"Ye . . . Yes," hesitated Angelito. Then suddenly he jumped up and rushed over to his companion.

"Friend of my soul!" he cried. "I can hardly realize that I am the accepted lover of your sister, that Socorro will be my bride!" He threw his arms about his friend's neck and kissed him on both cheeks.

The crippled youth smiled faintly as he accepted the bullfighter's caresses.

"My dear Angelito, I assure you your pleasure is hardly greater than my own."

"I can hardly comprehend it!" glowed the *torero*. "*Hombre,* a saint out of heaven would not be more welcome! To think of my amazing fortune!"

Rafael patted him on the shoulder and moved toward a chair at the table. The *espada* went on in his ebullient mood:

"*Caramba,* but I was a despairing man, Rafael. I was afraid we—er—sitting in the garden would prejudice the *Señora* against me."

"It did," admitted Rafael frankly.

"And the Señorita Margherita, too, I suppose— I could see that much last night."

"*Cá! Naturalmente,*" agreed Rafael drily.

"I saw that, so you can imagine how I spent the night, dear Rafael. *Diantre!* A night of torture. To fling away by my own act the most beautiful, the tenderest, the most virtuous . . ."

"My dear Angelito," laughed Rafael, "if you hadn't committed your indiscretion in the garden, you would never have gained *maman's* consent to your suit."

"I gained her consent by acting improperly!"

"*Seguro*—it forced her hand. You know the conventional penalty for such a fault is the marriage of the offending parties, Angelito, and it would never enter my mother's head to question that convention, to question the wisdom of giving my sister to a breaker of the rules of conduct."

"It *is* rather a queer punishment," admitted Angelito, who had never thought of it before, "to insist that a lover take what he desires. . . . Since you mention it, I wonder what your mother meant by that."

The poet waved a finger, "*Nada!* My mother meant nothing at all. She simply followed a convention as automatically as an insect follows its instincts. By the way, had you ever thought that the conventions of society and the instincts of animals are exactly analagous?"

"No, I hadn't, but your mother . . ."

"Oh, there is a convention here in Caracas that a youth and a maiden who have enjoyed dual solitude in a garden must marry. Why they should marry, how their marriage can cancel their indiscretion, that is a matter not to be questioned by a woman. It is accepted as a miraculous fact, like the Transubstantiation."

The poet's satirical flavor disturbed Angelito in

his new happiness. The suggestion that he had compromised Socorro in the slightest degree pained him. He wanted her to appear to the world as she appeared to him, adorned with a sort of celestial purity. A line of reasoning popped into his head to prove that she still retained her transcendental estate.

"But, *mire,* my friend," he began, "listen to this. If there is a convention that says two persons shall marry after certain things have happened, then that shows that Socorro has never really stepped outside of the conventions, for there is a rule governing her case."

The crippled youth began laughing again. "You really are in earnest about wanting my sister to be a paragon of propriety!"

"*Ciertamente,* Señor."

"I fancy you never had a sister."

"No."

"I thought not. They don't come like that. However, listen; I will give you a more comfortable way of looking at conventions than what you have. You place too much accent on conventions and too little on persons. You have observed that some conventions are a little flexible, as in your own case; why is that?"

"*Cá!* To save us suffering, I suppose . . ."

"Not at all. It is because the persons who break that particular convention are the most ardent, and therefore the most valuable individuals of our race. Their offspring will be the most vigorous and have the greatest share of the *élan vital* which propels life to its mysterious goal. So you see this whole disturbance is the very greatest compliment that could be paid you. Instead of holding the episode in regret, you should wear it upon your sleeve as a decoration."

"*Caramba!* What an idea! And did your mother think of all that? She must be the wisest . . ."

"My mother think of it! *Diantre,* no!" cried Rafael, amazed. "That is simply the rational foundation at the back of her instinct. She submits to it with ill grace and much complaining, but if I should tell her why she submits to it, she would think I had gone utterly insane."

"Then, *diabolo,* why does she—"

"My dear fellow, how does a bee fly straight to its hive after wandering and turning among flowers all day—women are the custodians of life. They divine its necessities. They sacrifice themselves, their kin, their loves, their ambitions and even their vanity at its behest. My dear Angelito, it is a miracle; it is the finger of God!"

The two men sat for some moments in silence. The bullfighter presently said, "I shall tell that to Socorro; it will make her happy."

The poet held up his finger. "Don't do it. Human beings, Angelito, are occupied mainly justifying their actions to themselves. A man always saves his face by reasoning away his sins; a woman dismisses hers according to how she feels. That is why every reconciliation between the sexes must be based on simple forgiveness. They have no mutual ground for explanations."

"I had better not mention this to Socorro?"

"No, she already feels perfectly at ease about her conduct. The best thing you can do is to assist her in forgetting it."

Rafael picked up the copy of *"Sol y Sombra"* which Angelito had dropped on the table and glanced idly through the paper. The bullfighter sat glowing over his suddenly changed prospects. Into what a family was he marrying! His brilliant brother-in-law; his heavenly wife; even his aristocratic mother-in-law! What a step up for a peon boy born in the slums of the Matadero! His pleasant musings were interrupted by an exclamation from Rafael.

"What is it?" asked the bullfighter.

"*Diabolo,* listen to this!" cried the poet, and in a voice trembling with wrath he began reading an article from the paper:

" 'A CALL TO PURITY!

" 'Aristocrats of Caracas, take heed! We have been too lax in our solidarity! We have been negligent guardians of the sacred blood of the old *Conquistadors.* Into that pure stream is draining turgid, bestial, peon blood that is stultifying our lineage, dulling our intellects, corrupting our manners and debasing our morals.

" 'Lacking in breeding, courtesy, *aplomb* and gentility, the social scum which chance has thrown into our midst does not hesitate to go to the extremes of indecency in order to force itself into matriomonial alliances with the aristocratic families of this city.

" 'Not long ago the writer of this article had the painful experience of seeing a certain peon who has gained some notoriety as a bullfighter in the *circo,* seated at midnight in a garden with a *señorita,* unaccompanied by any *dueña.*

" 'This young woman has hitherto been of the most honorable repute as well for her modesty as for her beauty and talents. Without doubt this scurrilous killer of bulls (it would be too great a compliment to call him a *torero!*) inveigled the young lady into this compromising position for the low and vicious purpose of forcing his marriage to the unfortunate *señorita;* a marriage which her family would never have countenanced otherwise.

" 'With such contemptible devices, fellow artistocrats, are the *canaille* intrenching on our racial purity. Such conduct is worse than seduction. Seduction slays one individual; mesalliances contaminate the race. Such unions should be ostracised by society and banned by our Holy Church.' "

During this passionate reading the bullfighter sat listening with vague comprehension and all he gathered distinctly was that a bullfighter sat in a garden with a *señorita* and this much of the phillipic came home to him with a certain familiarity.

"Who wrote it?" he asked.

"Who should write it," cried Rafael, "but Narciso Montauban!"

"What did he say about a garden?"

"Diabolo! He accuses you and my sister of sitting in a garden together at midnight!"

"Cá! That is a fact!" ejaculated Angelito uncomfortably.

"Fuego!" cried Rafael, striking the table with his fist. "What if it is a fact! Is Montauban to be allowed to publish every indiscretion my family commits?"

"Did he really say us—I didn't hear any names."

"He said a *torero* had induced a *señorita* to sit with him in her garden. You know everybody will know whom he is talking about!"

Angelito frowned, but in his heart he could not help feeling pleased at the distinction. Such a tale would cast a certain glamor over him in the *circo*. However, he frowned and growled out, *"Caramba, I am clear enough, but by good fortune your sister's name is not mentioned."*

"Hombre!" cried Rafael. "He couldn't have made it plainer. He says you are going to marry her, and that such a thing is worse than if she had been an indecent woman."

The bullfighter half rose.

"What! Socorro worse than a baggage!"

"Here he says it!" Rafael struck the paper.

"Socorro an indecent woman!" A sudden quaking wrath went through the bullfighter's powerful body. "May the lightning of God strike him dead! The stinking *samauri!* I'll go down and break every bone in his—" the peon started impulsively for the *calle*, his nostrils expanded, ready to smash his enemy. Rafael saw that he was really leaving the *casā* and limped rapidly after him.

"Here, what are you about?" he cried.

"I am going to the office of '*Sol y Sombra*' and smash that snake!" he cried.

"Stop, you can't do that!" warned the poet.

"Why can't I?"

"You can't go into a man's office and start an ordinary street brawl!"

"Hell's sacred devils, I can and I'm going to!"

"But Angelito, you'll disgrace yourself! You would be the butt of everybody's scorn! It isn't done!"

"But I am going to whip him! I'm going to smash him to bits—calling Socorro Jiminez a baggage!"

"That's all right, that's proper, but you'll have to challenge him formally. You can't go blundering into his office, breaking up the furniture, getting yourself arrested and dragged to the police court. You must challenge him as one *caballero* challenges another."

Angelito controlled his wrath with a sensation as of some one again checking his mighty muscles with the trivial threads of wont and custom.

"When will we get to fight?"

"Your seconds will arrange that."

"Now I'm going to fight him and kill him!" roared the bullfighter as if Rafael opposed it.

"You are quite right in that, Angelito. It will clear up your record as a man of honor and reinstate my sister's good name. Just how it does it, I don't know, but it does; another miracle, I suppose, like the loaves and fishes. Anyway, I'm glad to see you take that course. I had thought of challenging Montauban myself, but it's better to come from you."

"Yes, yes," agreed Angelito sharply, "that's right!"

"Now the question is, what arms are you the most skilful with, swords or pistols?"

The bullfighter came to a halt and considered. "I suppose I'm best with swords. . . ."

Chapter 12

WITHIN the next forty-eight hours all Caracas was gossiping about the article in *"Sol y Sombra"* and was speculating on the outcome of the Angelito-Montauban duel.

The bullfighters at old Malestar's wineshop predicted a swift disaster for the editor.

"The fight will depend," gesticulated Ercolito, pushing out a double-nine domino, "upon how long Angelito cares to play his man. He will lure him on for three or four rushes, perhaps half a dozen, then—pouf! It is a great pity, because Señor Montauban has talent and has given us all very good press notices . . ." Here the crowd began to speculate on who would be the next editor of *"Sol y Sombra."*

Among bullfight devotees in the downtown districts, the jeweler stepped into brief prominence because he had sold Angelito his plate. This gave him a certain authority on the *torero's* prowess as a swordsman.

"Caramba," he would shrug, "what chance has

an ordinary man against a trained athlete? Fighting skill is like all other skill, Señors, it comes with seasoning. Look at me in this business. If a diamond has a flaw in it, be assured that I will detect it at a glance. The years, Señors, the years fix us, fighter, editor, jeweler, what not. The years are like molds which enclose us ever so softly at first, but they become like stone."

"Perhaps it is Señor Montauban's way of committing suicide," suggested an old *caballero* with a skin like parchment. "He is young enough to prefer death to the loss of a *querida*. The young trip to death lightly, Señors, as if to their partners at a *baile*, but later, when death comes quite close and you can see his features . . ." The old gentleman lifted shoulder, brows, drew down his lips to deprecate such folly as seen from his maturer point of view.

In the Jiminez villa in Paraiso it was Señora Jiminez who was most often vocal. She pointed out to Socorro, to Margherita, to Rafael, innumerable times, what came of receiving a bullfighter into the family—an instantaneous challenge, a precipitate attack. Holy Virgin, he would be forever fighting and murdering men! They would never have any peace with such a member in their home!

"But, *maman*," Rafael would interpose, "he had provocation enough. Montauban wrote an article . . ."

Narciso write such a thing! She would never believe it! And if he did, did he not have provocation? For Socorro to give him the mitten like that! How he must have suffered! How he had loved Socorro! And now to be flung over for a bull-fighter who goes about flinging challenges without cause . . . here the Señora would weep in a peculiar manner, holding her face almost still so as not to wrinkle her smooth girlish skin, but with the tears trickling out of her eyes. She had practised this mode of weeping so long that she did it without effort. She was weeping for Narciso, whom she desired for a son-in-law, and whose standing in Paraiso would add prestige to her family. Now all her plans had gone awry on account of a peon bull-fighter! It was enough to make a good woman weep!

Socorro Jiminez avoided her mother's endless reproaches as well as she could by finding tasks in the sunshine of garden or *patio* which her delicately blooming mother carefully avoided.

The impending duel hovered like an incubus over

the girl's nights and days. It seemed unreasonable that Narciso Montauban was fighting over her. Such a thing was in character with Angelito, but Narciso . . . She couldn't understand it. She couldn't think what had come over him. In her imagination the two men fought all day long. She could see the big *torero* and the little editor making swift lunges at each other. And one would be killed, the editor of whom she was fond, or Angelito whom she loved.

The possibility that Angelito might be killed filled her with the utmost terror. She felt like going to Narciso and telling him that he must by no means hurt Angelito. It still seemed to her that she would have her old sway with him, that he would give up to her out of habit as he had always done. But her reason taught her that was untrue, that he and Angelito were actually fighting over her. Her innocent girlhood had somehow broken down and had dropped her into the black and tortured currents of life and passion whose very existence she had never suspected.

One noon the girl stood in the *patio* binding a new orchid to a piece of wood in order to root it, but her thoughts were plodding the treadmill of the duel. Presently Rafael came limping from his room. Socorro watched his painful walk and it filled her with pity. His lameness somehow had taken the edge off his youth.

As he paused to watch her fix the epiphyte to its host he said he had been over on Traposo *calle*.

"How is Angelito?" she asked, looking at her flower and coloring faintly.

"In the most insolent health, as usual."

"I mean is he uneasy about . . ." with a little gesture she signified the fight.

"Not as much as you are, I'm afraid, poor little *muchacha*," said the poet sadly.

"Then he is—a little?" asked the girl apprehensively.

"*Pues* no—*he's* not."

She looked at him suspiciously. "What do you mean saying 'he's not' like that?"

The poet paused undecidedly. "I hardly know whether to tell you . . ."

Socorro became alarmed at once. "You'll have to tell me now," she said in a low tone.

"*Sí-í, naturalmente* . . . the truth is I—I am a little disappointed in Angelito."

"*Anda!* How?"

"It's an odd thing. Still, it's simple enough

after you understand it. The fact is, Angelito is not a very good swordsman."

"Not a good swordsman . . ." She stared blankly at her brother. "That can't be, Rafael; an *espada* . . . not a good swordsman!"

"Yes, you see he has never used the rapier for any other purpose than in the bullring. He never took lessons with the foils. He—hardly had an opportunity. You probably know he was a poor boy." Rafael paused and presently added in a slightly different tone, "I thought I would better tell you."

The blood receded slowly from the girl's face as the full implication of her brother's preparation grew in her mind. She laid the half-bound orchid on a flower box. "Rafael, do you *know* he can't use a sword?"

"*Absoluto!* I carried down my foils to give him a little practice and explain a few little thrusts I know Montauban possesses, but," Rafael spread his hands hopelessly, "it was no use. He knew nothing about the foils at all. I could touch him at will . . ."

"Then Narciso will . . . kill him?" whispered the girl.

The poet made a helpless gesture. "Narciso may

possibly wound him and spare his life. I have always found him a generous fellow, but, of course, in an affair of this kind . . ."

The girl flushed. "Oh, Rafael, *don't* say 'affair' like that! It sounds so shameful!" She stood with a look of shame and distress in her face. "Why did Angelito go flinging out a challenge if he is not a swordsman?"

"*Pues,* it was sort of thrust on him in a way. When he read the attack on you in '*Sol y Sombra*' he leaped up and said he was going to throw Señor Montauban out of his own window. Of course, that was impossible. I told him a man couldn't . . ."

"Why was it impossible?" cut in Socorro. "That was the very thing to do!"

"Go in and raise a disturbance like a street brave?"

"Wouldn't that be better than getting killed?"

Rafael made an annoyed gesture. "*Caballeros* don't go about mauling persons with their fists; such a thing would be absurd, impossible."

Socorro gave up that point.

"Let's stop this duel, Rafael!"

"If Montauban would apologize . . ."

"Why couldn't Angelito apologize?"

"*Demonio,* Socorro!" cried the poet, outraged.

"Apologize because he resented an insult to you! *Huy!* He would far better be killed!"

"Madre in cielo!" gasped the girl, giving up this defense in its turn. "This is the most brutal thing I ever dreamed of! This duel is over me, but it doesn't give me a thought. Angelito goes out and gets killed to protect my honor! What good will my honor be to me if Angelito is killed?" Sudden tears stung Socorro's eyes.

The cripple put an arm about his sister. "Don't exaggerate your danger. I wanted to give you a little warning, so if Angelito was wounded it would not be too great a shock. He will hardly be killed. That doesn't happen often. Besides, Angelito is one of the most powerful and active men I have ever seen." He was inducing his sister to walk with him toward her room, but his instinct to philosophize impinged on his consoling attitude, for presently he added: "The difficulty is, Angelito has stepped outside of his class to live and marry. That is his real tragedy. Among all classes of society men fight for the women they marry. Some men here in Caracas fight with family prestige, some with their wealth, some with their art. The peons fight for their women by kicking and butting. You see, Angelito has climbed up into a new stratum, and when he attempts to mate he meets a new method of fighting, one in which he is not at all trained and at which he may possibly lose. He is under that natural handicap."

Suddenly the girl began to weep outright. "Oh, how horrible this is! How horrible! They think nothing at all of me; neither of them. I might be . . . an animal . . . a thing!"

"Are you really so neglected as you feel, Socorro?" mused her brother. "They are really helping you decide. A woman usually prefers the strongest."

"Rafael! You are outrageous!" She flung off his arm and went into her own room.

"Now isn't that characteristic," mused the brother. "Poor *chica,* to show her that all this is inevitable doesn't console her in the slightest degree. Somehow a woman can't lean back on mechanics and allow it to bear her where it will without hope or despair. No, there is something too vital about a woman to endure that. A woman is the *entrepreneur* of Life, and she will have nothing at all to do with necessity and death . . ."

Chapter 13

THE manner in which old Ana clanged open the grilled entrance of the blue *casa* and shuffled into the entry told Angelito that she was excited and angry and that she must have heard of his approaching duel. The bullfighter put down a foot to stop the faint oscillations of his hammock, where he swung between two columns of his *patio* and lay with narrowed eyes watching the entry. The next moment he saw his mother hurry in with her board of lottery tickets and immediately she shifted her physical haste into a verbal onslaught.

"This is what comes of running after fashionable *señoritas*—a fight! Getting disgraced in the papers! I have heard it! If you had been visiting a virtuous peon girl, but these silk-stockinged baggages, with half-a-dozen men hanging after them fighting and brawling . . ."

The *torero* sat up in his hammock abruptly. "Mother! Don't speak of Socorro Jiminez like that!"

"*Caramba*, it's true! The world knows what you did; it came out in the paper!"

The bullfighter grew intensely angry. "That's because the editor was cold mutton for her; trying to avenge himself by printing lies. But I've stopped him! He'll print no more of his filth after to-morrow!"

"God help you!" cried the old peon woman, aghast. "Are you going to kill a man on account of a demirep?"

The son leaped out of his hammock. *"Madre,* if you call that innocent girl a . . ."

"Demonio, isn't she! Didn't she go out in the garden with you at night and didn't her brother force you into the *casa* at the point of a sword and make you swear on the cross to marry her! Oh, I have heard it all!"

"God's lightning!" roared the *espada.* "Are they venting such damnable perjuries! I begged! I plead to marry her! She is an angel on earth!"

Old Ana's eyes widened in apprehension. "Pancho—you are not really going to marry her, are you—can't you give them the slip somehow?"

"I'll marry her if the saints preserve my life!"

Old Ana went into a fury. "A thousand devils! Bring such a fly-by-night into my *casa!* I'll not have it! I'll not endure it!"

A certain relief went through Angelito that this

subject was broached. "Very well," he agreed with
a little more composure, "I'll not bring her into
your *casa*. I suppose that wouldn't do. No
mother-in-law gets along with her daughter-in-
law."

"What do you mean; that I'm to move out?"
cried the old woman instantly. "I'll not move a
peg! You can't put me out! Surely, if there is
any justice in the laws, a son won't be allowed to
put his old mother into the streets!"

"No, I mean you may have this *casa* and I'll get
another. When I get a wife, naturally we must
separate, *madre*. You know we have never done
anything but quarrel all our lives. You beat me
when I was small and you quarreled at me since
I've been grown."

The old crone became furious again. *"Cá!*
You ungrateful son! All you remember are my
beatings and quarrelings. *Pues*, I remember getting up at night when you whimpered, patching
your shirts, and selling mangoes in the streets to
keep something in your belly. And now all I get
for my slaving is that I quarreled and beat you and
you'll turn me out of your home . . ." Tears of
self-pity filmed the old woman's eyes. "May the
saints forgive you, Pancho," and she turned away to

her own dirt-floored room at the back of the *casa*.

As the bullfighter watched her go, remorseful qualms seized him. He was moved to call after her that he was not turning her out of the *casa*, but would willingly go himself, nay more, he would put servants here to wait on her hand and foot. But to all this she shuffled silently to her room, her head wrapped in a coarse black mantilla, her board of tickets sagging under her arm. She was deeply wounded and would remain so no matter what he did or said.

Angelito drew a long breath of despair, and presently his thoughts came around to the duel he was to fight on the following sunrise. He knew by Rafael's manner that the poet was greatly disturbed about the outcome of the duel; but Angelito himself was not disturbed. Somehow he could not find it in himself to be apprehensive of the withered little editor. In fact, when the editor crossed his mind, spasms of anger twitched through his great muscles, his nostrils expanded, and the veins stood out in his neck, like the bulls he fought in the arena.

All the rest of the day the bullfighter's mood fluctuated between anger at Montauban, rapture at his approaching marriage, and distress at the idea of having to cast off his old mother. He tried to think of some way to house his bride and his mother together, but when he saw old Ana, going about with an obstinate expression on her old face and refusing to address a word to him, he knew that was impossible.

So in the afternoon he set off to look up real estate dealers and find a finer *casa* for his future wife. As he went about town a number of men spoke to him about his approaching duel and wished him fortune.

That night his duel occupied his mind to the exclusion of all else. At some hour he was startled by a knock at his door. He was afraid it was the police who had come to arrest him for challenging the editor. But it proved to be his mother. She stood in the doorway with her face in high illumination from the candle in her hand. She begged Angelito not to buy another *casa* and move away from her. Loneliness would kill her in this great house. She would be like a lonely old bat in a cave. She began weeping again and her old face was convulsed with grimaces. Between sobs she promised she would not scold any more, but would work in silence there in the *casa* as a servant for him and his wife. She said she would work for the aristocrats once more, as she had worked for them in her youth. For years she had been free from them, but now they would enslave her again. This *señorita,* she knew, was marrying her son for his money and she would fling it right and left after the fashion of unvirtuous women. . . .

So the old woman did her cause little good and much harm before she took herself back down the *patio* again.

There is a law in Venezuela, as in most countries, prohibiting dueling, but in Caracas there is a tacit understanding that duelists will not be molested at sunrise in a certain secluded level space beside the Guayra river just above the Puente de Hierro. The theory being, apparently, that the Caraqueno police are not up at such an hour.

So the early morning found Angelito and his second, a Señor Via, a quick-motioned little man whom Rafael had selected, en route for the conventional spot.

The Guayra river is really little more than a brook in the dry season, but its flood bed is very wide, and the Puente de Hierro, or Bridge of Iron, spans the whole valley at a great height.

The road which leads to this low dueling ground

beside the Guayra breaks away from the street at
the mouth of the bridge and leads down into a
banana truck farm. Through this rank growth
Angelito's cab followed a mere cart track with weeds
and flowers growing in the middle and on both sides.
This rural-looking road reminded Angelito of his
boyhood when he worked on the cacao *estancias*.
On just such roads he rode, a peon boy in the great
two-wheeled cacao carts, and now he was a *caballero*
in a cab with an aristocrat for his second, on his
way to fight a duel for the honor of a *señorita*—the
transition was magical.

Here the cab driver, peering down between the
vehicle and the horses said that another cab had
been along there this morning.

"The Montauban party," observed Señor Via,
drawing out his watch; "they are early; we are
prompt."

"I wish we had got there first," said Angelito,
feeling he had lost a certain point.

"That's of no consequence. And, remember,
you want to keep perfectly cool and collected during the encounter. Don't allow a slight scratch to
cause you to fling away caution."

"I think I have learned coolness in the bullring,"
remarked Angelito with a tinge of arrogance.

Sure enough, as they rounded the edge of the banana field they saw two cabs and four men on a level grass plot in the midst of the lush growth along the river bank. As Angelito drove up, this group of men bowed ceremoniously. The bull-fighter and Señor Via returned the salutations.

But even as Angelito bowed it struck him as a ridiculous thing to be bowing to a man he meant presently to kill. In the Matadero he had been accustomed to starting a fight with boastings, abuse and obscenity, not with bows. . . .

Señor Montauban's second had a case of dueling swords which Angelito could see were considerably shorter than the rapier used in a bullfight. The editor's second was a red-headed man who now approached Señor Via. The two seconds talked together a few moments, pointed toward the sunlight which filtered through the morning mists and chose the positions of their principals with reference to it. Then the red-headed man presented Señor Via with the case of swords who, in turn, brought the weapons to the bullfighter.

Both were exactly alike, delicate weapons with silver wrought hilts and slender blades. Angelito took up one, bent the point to the guard as a test, then accepted it. It was one of the handsomest swords he had ever seen.

"You will stand facing the north," directed Señor Via; "you will touch blades and then engage. Keep as collected as possible. Don't allow a scratch to irritate you. Now I believe the *caballeros* are awaiting on our convenience."

Señor Montauban and his second were advancing toward the middle of the dueling ground. Angelito and his friend went forward to meet them. The other three men, the two cab drivers and the surgeon, grouped themselves near the selected spot and watched silently with the keen interest such a spectacle provokes.

A certain feeling of unreality hung about the whole party for Angelito. It did not seem possible that the small, dignified, slightly bald man who was stationed opposite him with a sword could have written the scurrilous attack on him and Socorro. Nor did it seem he was really going to fight. Señor Montauban appeared too dignified to do either of these things. Angelito himself was not in the least angry. As a matter of fact, to fight a formal duel for a stated cause was far too intellectual a proceeding for Pancho Pachecho. Such a proceeding required an abstraction of which he was incapable. The bullfighter badly needed the stimulus of abuse, oaths, a buffet or two before he could begin really to fight.

The *torero* stood with his sword held a trifle high, as if he expected Señor Montauban to charge at him like a bull and impale himself on his blade. The steels clicked together and the two men fell into the peculiar doll-like poise of fencers.

For a moment Angelito stood feeling the strength of his opponent through his blade. It gave before his own iron wrist; the next moment he lunged rather awkwardly. Came a whisper of steel and his point passed harmlessly to the little man's side. The bullfighter recovered with great swiftness and lunged again. He passed over the little man's shoulder and at the same moment he saw a flicker of steel toward him and felt a sting in his upper arm.

Angelito sprang back with a little wave of surprise at the adroitness with which he had been pinked. But although he had retreated, Señor Montauban was just as close as ever. The editor's left arm and shoulder were swung behind him, giving the *torero* as a target nothing but the edge of a man.

It was with difficulty that the bullfighter parried his thrust. He tried to address his blade and lunge in return, but Señor Montauban kept pressing him back step by step and kept him parrying high, low, middle, face, legs, stomach. . . .

A certain rising anger grew up in the peon at this sharp and persistent attack. The editor was like a machine that went on perpetually driving him back and back. The *torero* had a feeling that his own sword was too long, that its point was useless. He made a sharp effort to leap back suddenly, get his sword tip down and drive in again. But his blade again encountered steel, it thrust off at an angle while a hot streak up his forearm told him that he had been touched again.

At this second sting and the sight of blood staining his sleeve, wrath seized Angelito. There was something monstrous and hateful in this absurd little wooden figure with its edge turned toward him. Now that Angelito was hurt, the wrong this little editor had done Socorro flared up again in the bullfighter's heart. Abuse, unspoken, was on the tip of his tongue and a pulse began beating in his temples. He poised his sword as if at an oncoming bull and lunged terrifically at the little man's heart.

His point slithered to one side, but the two men met, the bullfighter's momentum carried them several yards and at the same instant Angelito felt a keen pain through the heavy costal muscles under his arm. They were breast to breast, the point of the *torero's* sword thrust vainly into air behind his adversary, while Angelito was transfixed.

The next moment the bullfighter howled an oath, and like a flash loosed his sword and struck a full swing at the editor's jaw. Came a thud. The editor's hold on his own sword loosened, his slightly bald head flew back. The bullfighter lowered his mop of black hair and butted terrifically into the pit of the little man's stomach.

Came shouts from the seconds and the surgeon at the ghastly sight of a man stuck through by a sword, pounding, butting and kicking a helpless antagonist into insensibility. They rushed on him.

"*Diantre!* Stop him! Catch him! Hold him! The mad man!"

The three men grabbed and struggled with the wounded giant. He flung them off with a whip of his body and continued pounding and kicking his prostrate foe. In the scuffle one of the men got his hand cut on the sword sticking in Angelito's flesh.

"You damned *bribon!*" he howled. "What a cowardly attack!"

The red-headed second made a leap to get Angelito's sword and kill the bullfighter. Señor Via shouted not to do it, and succeeded in getting his own arms locked around the big fellow's neck, throttling him and hauling him backwards. Angelito was roaring and cursing them to let him alone, that he would kill the little imp of hell. In the midst of this his own second throttled his uproar and dragged him backwards. It took the three to hold him.

Montauban's second was in a rage. "This devil from hades! This mannerless wild man! It is our duty, Señors, as *caballeros* and guardians of fair play to kill this mad dog!"

Angelito's own second was crying: "You infamous wretch, attacking your opponent with your hands! What are you a *caballero* or a—gorilla?"

The surgeon was saying: "Here, you monster, let me pull that sword out of you! Are you utterly devoid of all human sensations?"

As the red mist cleared before Angelito's eyes, he saw Señor Montauban prostrate on the ground. He straightened himself and allowed the surgeon to approach him peaceably.

"The infernal little rat!" snarled the bullfighter. "I'll show him what it means to print his damnable articles about such a saint of a girl! I can whip an *estancia* full of such puny little aristocrats! I'm the best man in Caracas!"

He boasted and cursed and held himself stiffly against the surgeon who was pulling the steel from his side. The surgeon had poured iodine on the protruding blade so it would sterilize the wound as he withdrew it. The iodine felt to Angelito as if the surgeon were drawing a red hot iron through his flesh. He did not grunt, but he did stop his boasting.

All of the party were utterly disgusted with this attack on the editor outside the ritual; all except the two cab drivers who themselves were peons. These two winked at each other, made sharp striking gestures with their fists to show they were intensely pleased.

Señor Montauban did not need a surgeon; he was jolted and jarred, but did not have a scratch. Presently he revived, and, seeing the bullfighter's blood on his own clothes, asked if Angelito had wounded him. He seemed to remember nothing of what had occurred.

"No! No! You are not wounded, Señor," cried

the surgeon, "but you have been assaulted in a most cowardly and shameful fashion. It has been a disgraceful fiasco. I, for one, repent that I came out here at all. To call this spot the field of honor would be to expectorate on decency. The best all of us can do is to go back to the city and never pay the slightest attention to this yokel again!" He swung his head furiously toward Angelito.

The bullfighter was now beginning to be ashamed of his own violence. "He made me mad," he grumbled in faint extenuation.

"Caramba!" snarled the red-headed man.

The two parties climbed back into the cabs, but this time they were divided differently. Neither the surgeon nor the two seconds would ride with Angelito. They and Señor Montauban got into one cab, while Angelito and the two drivers used the other.

Chapter 14

By the time the morning mists had fully cleared away from the valley of the Guayra, polite society in Caracas was amazed and horrified at the conduct and upshot of the duel. Amazement came that Señor Montauban actually was a more skilful swordsman than the famous *diestro*, and horror at the brutal conclusion of the encounter.

By noon the most exaggerated tales of the duel were all over the city. Angelito, with his bare hands had maimed his rival for life. The editor's blade had pierced the *torero's* lungs. That the physicians and surgeons of Caracas were so outraged at Angelito's breach of etiquette that not one would dress his wounds, and now he lay slowly dying in the blue *casa* on Traposo *calle*. That Angelito was not dying, but that Señor Montauban would certainly challenge him again, and this time kill him. That Angelito had hopelessly disqualified himself as a *caballero*. And so, on and on.

By two o'clock, that is to say immediately after her siesta, Margherita Miraflores brought a selection of these versions to the Jiminez villa in Paraiso. A number of them were mutually contradictory, but with the ladies that did not shake their credibility singly or in the lump.

As soon as Margherita reached the Señora's door she began pouring forth her news in breathless Spanish.

"It was a terrible scene, Señora. Señor Angel was stabbed in a dozen places and a sword was sticking through his liver when he assaulted Narciso, and . . ."

The Señora dropped her embroidery. "Is he dead?" Her voice was ghastly.

"No, but he will die; all the surgeons in Caracas have refused to dress his wounds!"

"*Maria* in heaven—but why?"

"Because he *assaulted* Narciso!" The girl stressed the word with a sharp nod.

"But didn't they go out there to assault each other?"

"Yes, but he threw away his sword and beat him with his hands! He flung him on the ground and kicked him! And all with a sword sticking through him!"

"Through Narciso?"

"No, Señor Angel!"

"Holy Mary!" gasped the Señora, turning pale. "That sounds like some wild beast one reads about in African travels."

"Oh, the whole city is outraged at it! Everybody is talking about it and saying how shameful it is and what an insult on poor Narciso!"

"*Dios te oiga!*" cried Socorro. "To be flung on the ground wasn't half as bad as to be run through with a sword!"

"Socorro!" cried the Señora. "It's the insult of the thing! For that great bull of a *hombre* to be beating a *caballero* with his hands—suppose it had been Rafael, you can see that can't you? *Huy!* What an insult!"

"Every one says it was utterly indecent and must be avenged!" rattled Margherita viciously.

"How badly is Señor Angel wounded?" asked Socorro with a colorless face.

"Oh, badly; he can't get well," declared Margherita, instinctively, giving the worst news she had heard on the point.

"And his wounds are not dressed?" The girl arose excitedly.

"Now, Socorro," cried her mother, "you are not going down there!"

"Of course not, mother, but I want to get a doctor to him!"

"But the doctors won't go!" cried Margherita.

"*Pues*, I can send Rafael. He's clever about everything. He could dress a wound."

"*Que*, Socorro, I can't understand you! How can you consider resuming your unfortunate relations with that man when he has disgraced himself in a duel. Don't you realize that the whole city is holding him up to contempt?"

"*Absoluto*, every one is talking about it, Socorro," seconded Margherita. "Every one says Señor Angel's honor is gone. He is *sin verguenza*, and that he can't live over it no matter whether he gets well or not!"

"I don't care what they say!" cried Socorro. "He did the most sensible thing under the circumstances! If Narciso were sticking me with a sword I'd knock him over, too, if I could! Holy Mary, they were fighting, weren't they? I'm glad he beat Narciso! I'm glad! He's been needing a beating for a long time!"

"Socorro!" gasped Margherita.

"Daughter, what unwomanly sentiments!" cried her mother.

"I don't care, Narciso is a prig! I could beat him myself!"

"*Socorro!*"

As Socorro hurried into the *patio* toward her brother's room, she heard Margherita calling angrily after her: "Everybody says, *everybody* says . . ."

Señor Rafael Jiminez looked up at his sister's entrance, saw her face and immediately asked in a shocked tone, "Is he dead?"

"No, but you must go to his *casa* quickly, Rafael. He is badly wounded and not a surgeon in Caracas will go near him."

"What?"

"The doctors won't help him!" Tears filled Socorro's eyes.

Rafael dropped his pencil and looked at her. "Who told you such rot?"

"Margherita, just this moment!"

"Don't you know that's silly? A surgeon not go near a wounded man—a rich wounded man. Did she say why?"

"B-Because he—he picked Narciso up and flung him down during the fight!" gasped the girl.

"Did he do that?"

"Y-Yes, with a sword sticking through him. Oh, Rafael, it's horrible! And Narciso is going to challenge him again!"

Rafael got up and limped a little way from his writing desk. "Stop, don't jump at every wild tale you hear! That's a most absurd story!"

"But, Rafael, everybody says . . ."

"Says what?"

"That he's in disgrace and they'll have to fight again!" Socorro's eyes were full of tears and she bit her lips to keep from sobbing outright.

Rafael patted his sister encouragingly. "A lot of that is gossip. I'll go find out what truth there is to it."

"*Bien*, do go and see if he has a surgeon, Rafael."

"He either has one or doesn't need one."

"Are you sure?"

"Of course I am, Socorro. But that tale about Narciso going to challenge Angelito again—I'll look into that."

He started limping about his study, trying to find his hat, and Socorro, who had been calmed somewhat by her brother's manner of accepting the news, now started thinking on a less urgent but quite as painful a topic. She had several minutes for her

reflections, for Rafael's room was in disorder and
his hat was lost. When he found it and was nodding her good-by at the door, she asked in a small
voice: "Rafael, do—do you think he really was
dishonorable?"

"Who?"

"Señor Angel."

"Quite likely—what did he do?"

"Rafael!" reproached the girl, and then she repeated in a desolate tone that Señor Angel had
flung away his sword in the midst of the duel, leaped
at Narciso and butted him over.

The poet stood listening and gradually his composure gave way and he began laughing immod-
erately before her outraged eyes.

"*Huy!* Rafael! Rafael!" she cried.

"I can just see Narciso tumbling over," explained
the poet. "I know how shocked and amazed he
was."

"But was it *dishonorable?*" pressed the girl impatiently.

Rafael became sober and made a gesture. "Now,
my dear, what sort of honor do you mean?"

"Oh, Holy Mary!" sighed the sister, at the end
of her patience. "I might have known I could get
no sense out of you!"

But Rafael was not to be denied this philosophic point.

"*Pues,* Socorro, that is a very simple thing," he said gravely. "What we call honor is a term which means the rule of conduct in a certain locality among a certain class. Here in Caracas we have Spanish honor, peon honor, Carib honor, Negro honor. Before I could possibly answer your question you will be bound to tell me to what sort of honor you refer."

"You know I wouldn't speak of Carib or Negro honor."

"Probably not. I was simply giving you an idea of how many codes there were. When you analyze it, any code of honor is what a certain class of folk has found expedient to do under certain circumstances. When a man like Angelito comes up from one social sphere to another, a great many things which were honorable down below are considered dishonorable above; for instance, in a fight, peons butt with their heads, Spanish *caballeros* do not. I should say the essential ingredient of dishonor is originality or the element of surprise. Victorious armies have uniformly used dishonorable methods from the standpoint of the vanquished. Great financiers always have shady reputations. Successful politicians—but really that is too tainted a topic even to use as an illustration. . . . "

"Rafael," said Socorro, "from what you say I have no idea what you think about Señor Angel; I do wish you would go and see how he is getting on."

The poet perceived that his sister was not as interested in his reasoning as he was himself. He gave it up, went back to his writing desk, picked up a manuscript, put it in his pocket, and turned toward the door.

Socorro watched this act with evident disapproval. "Rafael, you are not going to read that to Señor Angel, are you? Remember, he is wounded already."

Rafael said he might strike up with some friend or other, and Socorro observed that he was "cold-hearted to think of such a thing under the circumstances."

Oddly enough, when he got outside the Jiminez lawn, Rafael hailed neither cab nor street car, but limped along the boulevard studying the pavement in deep thought. When he came to the Montauban château with its heavy and solemn Spanish architecture, he stood undecided a moment, then went inside.

Rafael Jiminez never entered the Montauban *casa* without a faint feeling of irony that such a gravely handsome structure should be wasted on such a man as Narciso Montauban. For Narciso to brood in such a nest and produce such an egg as *"Sol y Sombra"* was simple pathos. It was anticlimactical. "Now," he thought, "the poem I have in my pocket would be worthy of the height of these walls and the spring of this ceiling, but Narciso . . ." He shrugged very faintly as he moved along the great hallway of the château.

He found Narciso in a study which was as severely simple as the great noble rafters overhead and the polished syp floor underfoot were rich. The long narrow windows gave the study a somewhat monastic effect which Montauban's slightly bald head accented.

The editor of *"Sol y Sombra"* was apparently no whit the worse for the drubbing Angelito had given him. He sat at his great, flat, yellow writing desk on which were neatly arranged some papers, manuscripts and a pile of galley proofs. The journalist evidently was surprised to see Rafael, and the poet began a carefully prepared conversation by asking his former friend if he might tell him how shocked and grieved he had been at the appearance of the article in *"Sol y Sombra,"* and how deeply he regretted the rift between their families.

At this Señor Montauban's thin face paled somewhat, but he asked in an even voice if he might tell Rafael how shocked and wounded for life he had been when he and Rafael had blundered into the Jiminez garden on the most unhappy night of his existence.

As Narciso said this he did indeed look, to use his own Spanish hyperbole, "wounded for life." His sallow face had the thin, drawn look that comes from some continued strain. Rafael began to perceive vaguely something of the depth of his former friend's wound, a phase of the unfortunate affair which had heretofore escaped him because of a brother's congenital inability to conceive of any mortal man really having a tender passion for his sister. Now he suddenly felt sorry for the editor.

"I saw you were shocked, Narciso; so was I; but even at that I simply couldn't understand your article."

"You couldn't?"

"Frankly, no. I could not understand how a man could sit in a study like this and write such a thing."

The poet's old admiration for his study, his im-

personal attitude toward the insult thrown at his
family aroused in the editor some of his former
liking for his friend.

"The truth is, Rafael," said Montauban drearily,
"I don't understand it myself. The next morning
when I read my own article in my paper, I was
dismayed. It seemed impossible that I had written such a thing. That night I must have been
mad."

"*Ola! Ola!*" ejaculated Rafael, divining the
storm in his friend's heart and marveling that Socorro had caused it. He cast about for some way
to console his friend. "*Pues,* after all, Narciso,
this—er—misfortune at least will leave you more
leisure for your literary work. You did spend a
lot of time at our *casa*. I have often thought . . ."

"You mean my work on '*Sol y Sombra?*'"

"Yes."

The editor pushed away the proofs on his table
as if they were distasteful to him and arose.

"I am through with '*Sol y Sombra*'."

"You are what?"

"*Dios,* yes. I'll either sell the paper or let it
drop. I'm through. I never before realized what
barren, futile work it was; to spend one's life re-
cording the doings of illiterate peons who have

learned to stick a bull. What a beggarly occupation!"

The poet stared at him blankly. "What will Caracas do without a sporting paper?"

Señor Montauban made a gesture which meant it was no concern of his.

"What are you going to do yourself?"

"I don't know. I am thinking of going to Paris."

"For a permanent residence?"

"I think so."

Rafael, still with the intention to console, made a few vague suggestions about love and marriage, something about the biologic tendency of persons to marry their opposites; blondes, brunettes; tall men, short women; fat men, thin women, and naturally aristocrats, peons . . .

The editor did not seem impressed with this theory, for he said nothing.

"What I really dropped in to ask you, Narciso," said the poet, "is it your intention to—er—pursue the unpleasantness of this morning on account of what Angelito did?"

The editor's expression changed. "I have never before accepted a blow like that, Rafael."

"Still, a blow in a fight is not on the same footing as a blow meant as an insult. Besides, Narciso, you might have foreseen that Angelito would have reverted to his peon method of fighting if pushed to it. That was his reflex action when angered. It would be foolish to expect him to change his reflexes merely because he had a sword in his hand."

"The trouble with you is," said Señor Montauban drily, "you utterly destroy honor, will power, and self-direction with your mechanistic theories, Rafael."

"*Caramba!*" cried the poet rather touched. "Honor, will power and self-direction are all right as long as one doesn't mix the classes. But when you bring two men together who are fundamentally different, you might know there would follow a confusion of method, and that's dishonor. You ought never to have accepted a challenge from a peon, Narciso, and you certainly ought never to give one. Anything so formal as a duel is impossible between men of different classes; all they can do is fight." The poet bowed. "Now that is what I wanted to say, and I thank you for the courtesy with which you have heard me." Rafael started limping toward the door of the study.

Narciso followed him. "I am glad you came, Rafael; your conversation has been a pleasure to me." He hesitated and then added, "I wish, Rafael, you would tell your sister how deeply I have regretted my impulsiveness."

"I will explain it to her, Narciso; she is really a very generous girl, according to her viewpoint of life."

"I know she is—I know she is, Rafael. Sometimes I have thought that Socorro never did really care for me. I don't know, little things . . . but she is a generous girl."

As Rafael limped to the entrance of the château he felt a little pang of disappointment at not finding an opportunity to read to Narciso the poem which he had in his pocket. It did seem that his sister's rift with Narciso was an unfortunate affair for every one.

Chapter 15

BARRING the contingency of a challenge from Narciso Montauban, Angelito's affairs smoothed and straightened themselves into the commonplace raptures of a betrothal accompanied with passionate love. The bullfighter became a regular visitor at the Jiminez villa. Toward him the Señora's manner softened from open hostility into her original chill and disapproving courtesy. Margherita resumed her light and teasing friendship and occasionally Rafael called the *torero* into his study to hear his latest poem. Angelito hit on the device of listening to the verse, nodding solemnly and saying nothing. This gradually installed him in Rafael's estimation as a man of literary taste, "untrained, you know, but deep of heart . . ." The Señora scoffed at such a dictum; Margherita laughed at it; Socorro believed it and was not surprised.

Nevertheless, that Angelito had challenged a man and had been wounded in defense of Socorro's good name gave him a sort of standing even with the Señora. There is no way to satirize an act of this kind. It is as dogged a fact as money received, and cannot afterwards be denied.

Naturally enough the duel enhanced the bull-fighter's attraction for Socorro. She showered on the *torero* the blind prodigality of a girl's first full-blown affection. She was of an age when she should have had several such emotional experiences, but these had been precluded by the protracted and rather tedious courtship of Señor Montauban. During this period Socorro had thought at times that she was in love with Narciso, at other times she was sure she could never love any one. Angelito's unfortunate dinner caused her to reconsider this point, but it was not until her transfiguration in the garden that there burst on her the possibilities of delight that lay in her brain, body and whole nervous system; in brief, what one means by being in love.

It is true, since the night in the garden, Socorro's reaction to Angelito's caresses never reached such complete abandon except on the evening when he came back to her from the duel, wounded by Señor Montauban. Then the girl quite melted from tenderness and anxiety.

But at other times in her yieldings she now mixed a certain increasing intellectualism. She found herself setting right certain little mistakes Angelito made in his Spanish, and suggesting little differences in his deportment.

Nevertheless, each evening she awaited Angelito's coming with the utmost impatience and was displeased if he did not first come quietly around to the music room where she might have him for ten or fifteen minutes before she presented him to the family circle. His step on the walk, his tap at the window were quite enough to catch her breath, make her leap up and run to the side door where she could slip into his powerful arms.

As soon as Socorro's affection had reached this intimate stage she set about using all her influence to break Angelito's connection with bullfighting. She became chronically anxious for his safety.

"Light of my eyes," she would plead, "it is inhuman of you to torture me by entering the *circo*. Suppose something should happen to you!"

"But what else can I do, Little Heaven?" he would ask.

"What else? *Caramba!* What difference does it make whether you do anything at all or not?— you might write poems like Rafael."

"Holy San Michael, me write a poem?"

"I write a poem. . . ."

"Hm—yes—I write a poem."

"Rafael says you have talent. Then music, why not develop your music? Your guitar speaks a thousand voices to my heart."

"But, Adorable," he said, drawing her to him and smoothing her hair, "I have a great idea. I want to be the leading *diestro* of the world. I want to sail around the world with a great herd of wild bulls, like Juan Leon."

Socorro was horrified.

"But just think of it, traveling like a King through all the South American republics, going back to Spain, meeting the King himself, and you with me!"

"But how will you do it, *mi vida?*" asked the girl, beginning to be dazzled.

"By the reputation I make in the *corrida* with Juan Leon."

"But, beloved," cried Socorro, "you can't go into the *corrida* with your wound!"

"Oh, my dear, I am like tar; thrust a sword through it, draw it out, and the place heals instantly. Now feel here at this place in my side to see how nicely it has healed."

"O-Oh, Angelito—I won't do it!"

"Yes, do; it is cured!"

He took her hand and forced it inside his clothes to his wound and they slipped into each other's arms with the innumerable and protracted kisses of young lovers.

However, her anxieties always returned to Angelito's dangerous art, and one day she took the *torero* to Rafael's study to talk the matter over with her brother.

The girl laid the matter before the poet with vehemence and demanded that he show Angelito how wrong he was to continue in the ring.

As usual, the poet did not give the sort of advice his sister was seeking. He told Socorro if she hoped to preserve her present tenderness and passion for Angelito he certainly would better continue in the bullring.

The girl was astonished and indignant that Rafael should suggest that Angelito's profession had anything to do with her affection for him.

"I am fond of Angelito purely for himself," she insisted tartly. "Do you imagine his risking his life in the *circo* makes me care for him more keenly? It just makes me anxious and miserable, that's all."

"But your anxieties increase your emotions, Socorro," argued the poet with gathering impatience; "in fact, the danger a man risks is a sort of premium he pays on his love insurance."

"Rafael, you have chosen an ill time for a joke."

"Joke—that's not a joke! That's a trait built into all womankind. It is the foundation of romance. You will have to admit if you had never seen Angelito in the arena, you would never have been impressed by him in the first place."

"Perhaps not, right at first, but now . . ."

"There you are, you see it is in your blood. That trait was cultivated in you by hundreds of thousands of years during which man's chief occupation was fighting. If the old cave women had not acquired a taste for returned heroes, the world would have been given over to cowards and our race would have retrograded. So, for the man of to-day to hold the genuine passionate attachment of his wife there must be something risky in his occupation."

"What a shameful idea! Can't a woman love a man for himself alone? That's what every man and woman wants, love for their real selves!" She tapped her bosom impulsively. "Not for their wealth, rank, position, beauty, or anything but themselves."

The poet wagged a sardonic finger at his sister.

"Nobody has a real self in the sense you use it, Socorro. There is no one thing about you or any one else which is yourself. Every person is a plexus of innumerable influences; his clothes, wealth, language, appearance, social standing, the house he lives in, the clubs he frequents, his likes, dislikes, whims, crotchets, sense of humor, love of poetry or beer, are all factors in his repulsion or attraction for any other human being. All of these and a million other items are included in that very vague term 'self.' When a girl imagines she has any one concrete thing in her which is herself and asks to be loved for herself alone, she is talking nonsense. It is on a par with the belief in Santa Claus and all the other items in the mythology of childhood."

Socorro looked at Rafael vexedly. "Sometimes I wish I never had a brother like you! Occasionally you say a bright thing, but I never go to you for anything especial but what I get the silliest talk I ever heard. . . ." She stood looking at the poet in disgust and then broke out again: "The idea that Angelito here isn't one person! That he is like a bundle of sticks, take one stick away, his bullfighting, for instance, and maybe I wouldn't like him any more. I think the main reason you are so silly, Rafael, is because you never loved a human being in all your life."

The poet watched the two lovers go out of his study without saying anything more.

Chapter 16

WHEN at last the great Spanish *corrida* drew upon Caracas it subdued all other interests in the public eye. For weeks in advance it had been bruited in the pages of *"Sol y Sombra"*; now leading articles appeared in the graver dailies, *El Diario, El Tiempo, El Expreso,* in which were discussed the art of Juan Leon; the esthetics of tauromachy; the correlation between Spanish civilization and the bullfight.

El Tiempo printed an interview with Juan Leon in which he discussed the movement in Spain to suppress the bullfight. "This movement," said the famous *diestro*, "marks the beginning of decadence in the Spanish spirit. A bullfight is the most beautiful spectacle that can be imagined—emotion, art, courage, light. The Greek people, the most artistic people of all history, beheld their hero of tragedy die and were all the more fond of him because he converted grief into artistic material. Formerly we Spanish, too, were like that. A *torero* would die in the ring and the fight would go on, for we were a strong nation and, above all, artistic. Now the decadents are seeking to subvert tragedy into sentimentalism and drown the courage of a nation in their tears."

"Sol y Sombra" flamed out in color with photographs of Juan Leon and Angelito draped with the Venezuelan and Spanish flags. The caption read: "Separated by the sword of Bolivar and Montillo; united by the art of Angelito and Juan Leon."

Posters of the coming *corrida* lined every *calle* from Candelaria to Calvario. Brass bands were likely to break into full blare around any corner adorned with streamers of the coming fight.

At the *biblioteca* all the back numbers of the Madrid and Barcelona papers were ransacked and their students could speak with authority upon Juan Leon's style. Because bullfighting is the most stylistic of sports its fashions vary from season to season. Now it is the suave and courtly style that receives public applause; then it is a languid and indolent address (a pure affectation, naturally, as if an *espada* would be negligent with a bull charging him). Then there is the acrobatic style of which Angelito was a master. All this information was rehearsed in preparation for the proper intellectual enjoyment of the coming fight.

Indeed, the tour of a great Spanish *espada* with a herd of fighting bulls through South America is unlike any North American spectacle. It has all the flair of a circus; all the éclat and wide advertising of a championship pugilistic contest; it is more dangerous than football; it has the stir and color of a horse race; the grace and music of grand opera, and the ineluctable fatality of tragedy.

Yet it is more sincere and solidly founded than any or all of these. It is because the fatal event in tauromachy is real and not feigned that gives it its tremendous hold on human emotions.

It is art, because it does what all art strives to do, gives a swift comprehensive epitome of life within a period of time brief enough for the whole drama to be felt without loss of strength or blurring of impression. Indeed, the bullfight is the most perfect presentation of life yet devised by art. It is a presentation of life itself and is not a mimic show. It encompasses the strong permutations of fortune, and at the end a real death broods over the arena either for the *torero* or for the beast. It is sensuous, terrifying, dazzling and fatal. In the midst of intense color and movement it forecasts the end. It is pregnant with the austere and beautiful truth that the fitting end of life is death, that the feverish round of our days is held in the bosom of eternity. It eases the petty raptures and anguish of its own spectacle against the dark infinitude of nothingness.

Chapter 17

AN increasing anxiety had hung over Socorro Jiminez during the approach of the great *corrida,* but now, since it was here, this gave way to the kind of exultation which a great fête always brings. It was as if the fanfare which greeted the *representación* had such a glowing ornamental superstructure that it made the girl forget the tragic reality which lay at its heart.

On the morning of the *corrida* the boulevard in front of the Jiminez villa was already bright and vocal with packed street cars, cabs, and groups of pedestrians flowing cityward to the *circo*.

A traffic policeman was stationed under the banyan in front of the Jiminez villa giving drivers and motorists instructions as to what streets were clear to the destinations they sought.

Through an open window, Socorro Jiminez watched the endless and colorful crowd flow past the iron fence. The vertical bars gave each passing group the design and composition of an oil painting. She might have been looking on some very vivid mural decoration.

The pageantry of the scene brought to Socorro's mind the possibility of her future husband becoming a great *diestro* in Spain. The thought aroused in Socorro's heart that vague longing for Spain which sleeps, like a racial nostalgia, in the bosom of every South American. The wife of a great *espada* in Barcelona, or Madrid! What a change from the provincialism of Caracas! Ancient, tawny Spain. . . .

A cab drew up at the gate and a moment later Margherita came running up the walk shaking her handkerchief at her friend.

"Isn't this a wonderful day! Old Tomaso could hardly drive up here. The whole street was coming against us. If any one should fall down in the street he would be dragged straight into the *circo!*"

Margherita hurried in and embraced her friend rapturously. "What are you going to wear?"

The Señora entered from the rear, holding an old rose dress in her hands. "I don't know whether to wear this or my new frock from Paris. . . ."

"Oh, that, that, Señora! We must be brilliant to-day with a member of our family in the *corrida*. You must admit Señor Angel gives us ton . . ."

"For to-day at least," added the Señora, not altogether displeased. "Now, Socorro, do turn around and decide what you are going to wear!"

With a lingering look out of the window, Socorro gave herself up to a consideration of gowns. But what loads and loads of people were passing the villa. It seemed to her a sort of long-drawn-out tribute to the skill and bravery of Angelito.

By eleven o'clock all the numberless cafés of Caracas were jammed with diners, eating betimes for the *corrida*. Postcard venders moved among the tables offering the usual obscene pictures for sale mixed with portraits of the popular fighters, Juan Leon, Angelito, Ercolito. Out in the *calles* the peons were sowing sucked orange rinds and gnawed mango stones all over the cobbles. A liberal sprinkling of Englishmen and Americans towered above the crowd; oil promoters mostly, some of whom had come from as far as Maracaibo or Callao on the Coroni to see the one all-absorbing spectacle of the season. These big fellows were offering prodigious prices to rebuy box seats, all of which had been sold days before.

In old Malestar's wineshop, among the tables reserved for the *cognescenti* went on a myriad-voiced discussion. How did Juan Leon's bulls compare with those of the great Taglione of the preceding season? *Diantre*, Señor, more magnificent than ever! These bulls were unreasonably superb!

The attendance would undoubtedly top all previous records. There were sure to be *mujers* and *muchachas* suffocated in the jam!

An old gentleman suggested they would best get across to the *circo* while it was possible to cross the streets.

"What is the hour, Señor?"

"Twelve fifteen and they say cabs and motors already have to stop two blocks away and the passengers walk in."

The old *aficionados* sat and listened with thrills to the continual uproar outside. What a *representación* they were about to witness!

The statement that no cab could approach within two blocks of Nuevo Circo was not quite true. At that very moment a cab containing Rafael and the three ladies of his house had succeeded in getting into the edge of the great plaza fronting the *circo*. Here Angelito stepped out of a shop and met them in accordance with a prearranged plan. Then with Angelito in front, Socorro next, the Señora, Mar-

gherita and Rafael in order, the five threaded their
way across to the great façade, glaring red in the
light of high noon.

The quintet held to each other's arms and moved
along with their faces tipped up as pedestrians do
in a dense throng. They were looking at the great
entrance ahead of them and the inscription over it,
"Sol y Sombra." Socorro clung to Angelito's arm
in the wide noise of the crowd and read the inscription.

"Oh, carissimo!" she called. "How I hope it
will bring you *'Sol'* and never any *'Sombra.'* "

The bullfighter turned and smiled in her eyes.

"It has been a mother to me, *mi vida,* this place,"
and he motioned a free hand toward the pile.

The girl knew what Angelito meant, that all his
position and wealth, yes, even their own exquisite
passion, was a child of this lurid building. Even
in the hot press, the girl felt a thrill of profound
gratitude that this great building had given her her
lover. How different Angelito was from what she
used to fancy when she saw him in the ring! How
much more lovable. The glamor of his fighting was
now the least of his endearments for her. He was
so thoughtful of her and he awakened in her raptures she had never imagined. The grim walls of

the *circo* had mysteriously bestowed upon Socorro womanhood, love and a subjective life as keen and brilliant as the spectacles of the arena itself. It had opened to her two queendoms, her emotions and the world.

One of those little feminine outbursts broke on her out of her thoughts, and she pressed the back of the bullfighter's hand to her bosom.

"Can you feel your side at all, *alma de mio?*" she asked anxiously.

"Not at all, *carissima.*"

They were to the entrance now. Here Angelito must deliver the ladies to Rafael's care and go around to the bulls' gate in the rear of the *circo*. As he pressed Socorro's hand in farewell, the girl's face whitened suddenly, her bosom rose and fell sharply; she lifted her arms about his neck and kissed him passionately, pressing her lips to his in three distinct impulses as she did when they were alone. Even the Señora made no remark at this; indeed, the other three of the party appeared not to see them. As for the crowd, jammed cheek by jowl with them, they were utterly blind to everything except what was lifted high above them, like the brazen calf of Israel.

Angelito waited at the entrance for Rafael to return and tell him where the family had found their box so he could throw them his cloak. When the poet came back he was smiling.

"We are only two boxes removed from the press box," he laughed. "Narciso has just paid us a box call. He said he was leaving Caracas next week and wanted to be friends again. I am glad of the reconciliation, Angelito. Montauban is really a good fellow, and among all of us, I really believe he has suffered the most pain."

With the kisses of Socorro Jiminez on his lips, the bullfighter went around the long circular wall of the arena and passed the ambulance and horses standing at the bulls' gate and never once observed them. A little later he stood in the hot sunshine before the gate, knocking for admission.

The *monosabio* who opened the gate for Angelito wore a shirt of red silk instead of the usual cotton, and this unaccustomed splendor marked the magnificence of the occasion.

Angelito stepped into a small enclosure walled off from the arena. In this hot, open space stood a pair of shining black mules with red harness. These animals tossed and snorted, rendered uneasy by the faint stench of dried blood which hung in the hot air.

To the right the mouth of a dark tunnel sloped downward to the bull pits where were stabled six of Juan Leon's shipload of Spanish fighting bulls. Next to this tunnel was the door of a dressing room, and next to this, a door with a cross carved on it. This was the entrance to the chapel in which the fighters would presently hear a mass before beginning their hazardous games.

Beside the chapel door, in the shade of the overhang, Father Ignacio in cassock and round priest's hat, stood talking to a man a trifle shorter and more compactly built than Angelito. This man wore a well-groomed look of success which caused Angelito to ticket him, automatically, as some wealthy amateur whose curiosity had led him to accompany the priest behind the scenes of a bullfight.

He was still speculating on the fellow when Father Ignacio glanced around, saw who had entered and held out an arm toward Angelito as he continued to talk to the stranger.

"Come here," invited the priest. "I want to present you, Señor Angelito, to Señor Juan Leon of Barcelona. Señors, I cannot express my pleasure

at bringing together the foremost artists of Venezuela and Spain."

Angelito was utterly taken aback to find this
man was the famous Juan Leon. The two *toreros*
bowed low.

"Señor Angelito, I have heard of him long before I reached these shores. I am very proud to
meet a brother artist whom I have been looking
forward to see."

Angelito said that he anticipated much pleasure
in seeing Señor Leon demonstrate the latest Spanish styles in bullfighting. Angelito said all this in
very good Spanish indeed and thought that his
well-worded reply was partly due to Socorro. She
had lifted him up on another plane. It was impossible to be associated with Socorro, to love
Socorro, and not become a *caballero* indeed. With
this feeling of having stepped into a new and finer
world, Angelito opened the dressing-room door and
bowed Juan Leon in before him.

The dressing room was cut up into small compartments, each one tiled in white and furnished
with electric lights and a shower bath. Fans kept
up a constant droning, and, while the air of the
room was extremely damp, the circulating air made
it not too uncomfortable.

For the first time in his life Angelito had a feeling of ownership in these appointments. Heretofore he had an impression that he was a peon interloping in a tiled bath; this gave way before the fact that he was to marry Socorro Jiminez.

He stepped into his own compartment where waited an attendant to help him. His green fighting clothes were laid out on one side and made a pleasant contrast against the white tiled background. He stripped briskly, and, as is the way with powerfully developed men, he appeared larger without clothes than with them. He bathed and his helper began taping his feet, winding the sticky stuff in and out between the great toe and the next, making a firm, tight plaster around the ball of his foot, then cris-crossed back to the heel. As the fellow worked, he talked: The bulls in the pit below were wonderful; never had he seen such animals, hair like silk, molded muscles, horns not spreading like the creole bulls, but sharp and black. The attendant kept praising the Spanish bulls as if they had been his sweetheart.

Angelito got to his feet and lifted himself lightly on his toes, trying the set of the tape. It was all right. The fighter sat again, the helper picked up the green stockings and slipped them over the somewhat square-molded calves of the *espada's* powerful legs. Then Angelito drew on his tight-fitting fighting slippers and green velvet knee breeches. About the knees were buckles and these the helper drew tight, with all his strength, under the abiding belief of the *circo* that the more tightly bound were a fighter's knees the more agile he was.

As Angelito dressed a droning from the arena filtered into his dressing room. Then the cadence of a band came to the fighter's ears, softened by the walls of his compartment. It sounded like a distant silver voice of exquisite flexibility gliding through the strains of a waltz.

It pricked up Angelito's nerves. For him, the *corrida* had begun. He hurried on his green silk scarf, adjusting one end to his waist and turning himself slowly and carefully, winding the tough silk around him, fold on fold. He tucked the end in and then put on a tight green jacket of waist length encrusted with gold embroidery. Then he walked out of his compartment with a springy feeling in his tightly bound knees and in the unyielding hoof-like tape about his feet.

A moment later Señor Leon joined him. The Spanish *torero* was in black. Angelito had never before seen a black fighting regalia. It struck a note of dignity, almost of austerity. Out of the other cubicles appeared the *banderilleros* and *mono-sabios*, the ring attendants and the mule driver. All were as colorful as a masque. When the *mono-sabios* thought their elders were not looking they flipped at each other with their handkerchiefs. Then the whole procession filed out of the dressing room and went into the chapel.

The chapel of the *circo* was a little larger than the dressing room and a little warmer on account of the candles burning on the altar. On the right side glowed the perpetual little oil light in its ruby bowl. Its tiny red flame burned in the gloom now a little brighter, now a little dimmer. The *toreros* stood at prayer because their bound knees would not permit them to kneel. At the altar Father Ignacio bowed at the appointed intervals to kiss the book which an altar boy presented to him.

Angelito kept his eyes fixed on an effigy of our Lady of Sorrows and it seemed to him, in the wavering light of the altar candles, that the eyes of the virgin moved ever so slightly and her uplifted hands beckoned ever so faintly in signal that his prayer for safety in the coming *corrida* was answered.

"Most Holy Virgin," murmured the brilliantly clad fighter, "guard me once more in the arena.

Protect me from the horns of the bulls and guide straight my rapier. Preserve me, Most Blessed Lady, save me . . . " His murmuring died away into an unworded emotion of supplication to the small white figure high up on the altar to save him from the perils of the fight. He crossed himself, touching his forehead, lips and chest with his fore-finger, middle finger and ring finger and kissing his thumb nail.

Chapter 18

WHEN Angelito came out of the chapel the sensuous swing of the band broke on his ears, its pulses accentuated by the ironic chirring of the castinets.

Inside the small enclosure the procession of the bullfighters fell quickly into line, each man taking his place through long established custom. The *toreros* swung their long brilliant cloaks over their shoulders. Juan Leon used a cloak the color of old gold which made a striking color scheme against the black of his fighting suit.

The *monosabios* made a red and blue queue to the line of fighters and at the end came the mules with the red harness. An almost vertical sun beat up out of the ground the stench of blood where thousands of bulls had been dragged out of the arena. The fighters drew out their perfumed handkerchiefs and blurred as best they could this penetrating odor. A lad in the rear of the line lifted his snub nose and blurted out, *"los pies de mi padre,"* and all of the boys and some of the men began laughing.

With a flourish the music in the arena ceased. The fighters straightened their line, sighting ahead of them and calling sharply for some individual to step in or out. They set back their shoulders ready to step off. The band crashed into a military measure; the big double doors in front of them opened; the men swung forward.

An immense cheering broke from the multitude and burst on the incoming procession almost like a continuous physical force. The gala colors in the enormous amphitheater, the glare of the sand, beat down and up into Angelito's eyes. The tumult was composed mainly of the name "Juan Leon," boomed over and over. Now and then he could distinguish his own name and occasionally that of Ercolito. He was distinctly second, and he registered, in his own mind, that when this *corrida* was finished he would be first. At intervals the music of the band reappeared among these billows of applause like foam spangling the waves.

The fighters began their long march around the great circle, and as they went the applause nearest them stepped up into a frenzy of shrieking, screaming, whistling, waving hats, sticks, parasols, handkerchiefs. The procession might have been hot and made the spectators close to it boil.

A passion to make the most of this unexampled opportunity poured strength through Angelito's body. His heart beat. He moved along swinging his green cloak from side to side. He was self-conscious from the fact that he meant to be the leading *diestro* of this great day, but even at that his movements did not lose the cat-footed grace of a bullfighter. Above all, he wanted Socorro to see him. He marched around with his eyes leaping from box to box ahead, trying to find her. She was within two compartments of the press box, but that was hard to find in an endless repetition of boxes, all in violent agitation.

In the circuit, out of custom, Juan Leon paused in front of the draped stall of the President of the Republic. The President was a rather fat old man of military bearing with decorations across his chest. Juan Leon swung off his yellow cloak and flung it up to the box. The bullfighter's sudden change from brilliant yellow to black made the amphitheater gasp. The President's wife leaned out, caught the cloak and flung back her handkerchief. The Spaniard bowed low over the filmy bit of lace, and placed it in the brocaded frog of his jacket, a white spot that relieved his somber costume.

Then the other fighters went about throwing up their cloaks, red, purple, orange; the circling balustrade took on the color of the iris.

Angelito went two boxes beyond the press box when he discovered Socorro was not there. A trepidation seized the fighter lest he should miss her. Then he saw her leaning over the balustrade and waving at him. He had passed her lodge, the second stall on the near side of the press box. He walked back past Señor Montauban and shot up his cloak to her eager hands.

At this all the preliminary players spread out over the yellow ring to receive the bull. The uproar of the amphitheater sunk to attention. From the topmost round of the great bank of seats came the military call of a bugle. It rang out a clear single voice informed with man's age-long defiance of danger and wounds and the inimical powers of nature. It was a dauntless voice. It was the cry of man facing the universe, courageous, self-dependent and pagan.

When the bugle ceased the silence became absolute. Angelito stood at the barrier under Socorro's box looking fixedly at the door of the bull pen. Above it, on the great cinema platform, stood a man with rosettes in his hands. The door beneath him opened. A bull's head emerged from the black rectangle. The man above lifted his darts and flung them downward with all his might. The beast leaped forward with the crimson rosettes glowing against his black shoulders. The sheer beauty of the powerful silken animal sent a thrill of admiration over the *circo*.

Instantly the brightly clad players fell into movement with their scarlet capes. The arena became a bewildering maze of color. Like a black bolt, the bull launched himself at the nearest of his provokers. Other players wove in between the bull and the object of his rush, drawing the beast's charge from one player to another. The great black animal lunged among them in a perpetual curving, tossing rush. The men scattered before him like so many brilliant birds. The fighters ran lightly, waving their red capes, advancing, retreating, leaping aside from the bull with the effortless ease of athletes. It was the most graceful and limpid movement of the bullfight.

Came a scattering of *"Oles!"* and *"Bravos!"* from the seats. Angelito stood beside Juan Leon at the barriers. Several times the play brought the bull within a few yards of the indolent *toreros*, but neither stirred their position nor moved a muscle, but studied the bull as he lunged past. Indeed, this passing of the bull close to the undisturbed *toreros* brought little gusts of applause from the audience. Juan Leon, leaning against the barrier, was more admired than the *banderilleros* in full play.

Once or twice Angelito looked around at Socorro and presently caught her eyes. Her beautiful face was filled with animation. She seemed to repeat the question of the whole amphitheater, "What sport in the world is comparable to this? What grace, what light, what gay skirting of peril!"

By concert of the players the bull was drawn to the center of the arena and then the actors suddenly danced away and the bull was left pawing sand over its back, ready to lunge instantly at its most conspicuous foe.

This was the end of the first scherzo movement of the sonata of the bullfight.

A man in blue silk with crimson *banderillas* in his hand now advanced holding his red darts toward the animal and waggling them tauntingly. A Venezuelan bull would have required much more provocation than that to be lured into another charge, but the Spanish thoroughbred flung himself instantly, and with amazing velocity, at the *banderillero*. The man held his two red darts straight up toward the sky, balanced himself a-tiptoe and leaned forward in a slow fall toward the charging bull. With a full arm swing he brought the keen tips of his darts down into the brute's shoulders at the precise moment, apparently, when the animal plunged black horns into his unprotected stomach. But with the down stroke of his darts, the *banderillero* swung his body aside; the upthrust of the sharp horns touched nothing at all. The great bulk of the bull brushed aside the fighter's outstretched arms, and the animal dashed past with two new crimson torments dangling in its shoulders and whipping back and forth with every lunge.

The man was already flying for the *contrararias*, and he leaped inside the small opening just ahead of the bull's horns. Another *banderillero* in purple with yellow darts approached from another quarter. He went through the same play, lifting his weapons, leaning forward striking, swerving aside and dashing for safety. This one could not gain one of the small entrances and he vaulted over the barriers apparently not an inch from the bull's horns.

Everybody was shouting and laughing at the close squeak. From the direction of the cheap *"sol"* seats of the arena came a spearman in blue. The bull turned on him with undiminished fury.

Shouts of *"Ole toro!"* "Brave Bull!" "Noble Bull!" went up from the amphitheater at the animal's persistent heart.

Quite near Angelito in a box, two companions, apparently a Venezuelan and an American, were shouting to each other above the applause.

"It's a splendid bull!" cried the Venezuelan to his American guest. "He stands the steel well!"

"It's too cruel!" complained the American, who was evidently considering the three pairs of *banderillas* stuck in pairs down the shoulders and the blood that reddened the whole forepart of the animal down past the knees.

"Cruel, la, the bull doesn't mind that, *mi amigo;* he is angry! Do you mind a wound when you are angry?"

"But look at him, he is trying to shake the darts out!"

"Cá, yes, but in another moment he will forget that pricking!"

The *banderilleros* who had been playing the bull now came trotting in from the arena with sweaty faces and heaving breasts. It seemed odd that men in such gay silks should be hot and sweaty. Their bright colors somehow suggested an invincible buoyancy. At the same moment one of the *mono-*

sabios came running along the aisle between the
barriers and the boxes with a number of rapiers in
his arms. The boy hurried out through the *contrararias* and offered his blades to Juan Leon. The
Spaniard selected one, drew its slender blade from
the scabbard, whipped it in air, then glanced cour-
teously at Angelito as if asking permission, and
spread a red silk cape over the rapier, using the
blade as a flagstaff.

A burst of renewed applause boiled around the
amphitheater at the entry of the famous Juan Leon.
This was the beginning of the third and final movement of the bullfight. The Spaniard advanced
through the brilliant sunshine, a solitary black figure with the crimson cape against the infuriate bull.

Angelito watched him with the critical eyes of
a fellow artist, but there was something so simple
and disarming in the great *espada's* approach that
he won even Angelito's sympathy.

Juan Leon had that peculiar pervasive possession
called personality. That is to say that about the
man clung a symbolic quality so that his adventures
became the immediate and singular adventures of
every person who beheld him. The great circular
bank of seats sat breathless, gazing fixedly at their
alter ego as he walked out on the yellow sand against

the bull. His courage entered their hearts and became their own. Indeed, for the passing moment he was the object of the throng's great and passionate love, because it was their self-love.

The bull glared at this solitary adversary. The black fighter waved his sword and crimson cape at the animal. The next moment the thoroughbred flashed at him like a black thunderbolt, and the whole audience was struggling spiritually in the midst of the fight.

The great Spaniard managed his bull with astonishing technique. With dextral and sinistral passes of his silk he seemed to swing the furious bull to left or right by some magic force of will. The amphitheater roared; they were conquering.

Turning, backing away, evidently at ease yet intensely alert, the great *espada* conducted his raging enemy in a great circle about the arena. He was somehow making the very most possible of the bull.

Suddenly the aristocratic *"sombra"* section of the *circo* realized what Juan Leon was doing. By means of his quiet and finished technique he was subordinating himself to exhibit the grace, the speed, the strength and monumental lines of the bull. Came a swift picture of the great black brute

charging, horns leveled, head down; now the tremendous up-toss under the whip of red silk; now
a front view of square chest, the lines up the bulg-
ing black neck leading to the whipping *banderillas;*
a side view of flying legs and blood-washed shoulders, black against crimson, a repetition of Juan
Leon's own costume and the cape he carried; a
rear view of lashing tail, immense propelling
haunches and swinging parts. The *diestro* forced
from the spectators a sharp admiration, a passionate understanding of the sculptural energy of the
brute. He exhibited the prince of fighting animals
in the moment of its greatest fury. The drama
passed beyond the bounds of an event in flesh and
blood. It breathed an immortal beauty. This
charging bull was one with the Discobolus or the
group of Laocoön. With the solidity of a statue it
blended the color of a painting and the movement
and suspense of drama.

In the midst of this play the bull came to a stand.
A typhoon of applause beat in from the amphitheater. The *espada* unwrapped his rapier. Its
slender glint looked absurd against so huge a foe.
Yet with it Juan Leon would bring into the spectacle that which all other artistic forms have either

mimicked or eschewed, the passing of life, the infinite suggestiveness of death.

With sword bare, the *espada* walked directly toward the ponderous bull. The animal faced him. Leon lifted the hilt of his rapier level with his eyes with its tip depressed toward the little vulnerable spot between the brute's shoulders. He stood a composed black figure with a wisp of steel. He stamped his foot at the slavering animal. Instantly the red-splotched bulk hurtled toward him. With hilt held high and point down he leaned forward. From the moment the tip of the thread of steel touched the crimson shoulders, the bull's horns had perhaps thirty inches to go to rip open the *espada*. But the great black head never traversed that space. The shining steel sank into the shoulders. The bull slowed swiftly as if checked by an invisible buffer in the air. It came to a halt. It shifted its powerful legs in an effort to stand. It swayed a little. Its foreknees folded gently on the sand; then its haunches settled down as if to sleep. A moment later the animal rolled over dead.

The *circo* applauded as deliriously as if every particular hand in the amphitheater had held the rapier. Above the tumult sounded the clear triumph

of the bugle announcing the death of the bull. At
the south end of the arena the gates were thrown
open and in jingled the black mules in their gay
harness. They trotted across the arena to the dead
body, hitched a chain around its horns and dragged
it out, leaving a furrow in the sand.

The band struck up a blithe air. *Monosabios*
hurried out with spades and buckets to fill up the
furrow, to level the bull's tracks and to scoop up
the dung the animal had dropped in its torments.

Joyousness filled the amphitheater because every
spectator had faced down death with glorious courage. All were heroes in Juan Leon.

Out of their enthusiasm, out of their self-love,
they flung down coins, jewelry, gold cigarette cases.
A rain of valuable gewgaws sprinkled the sand.
The throng adored their alter ego. They were
throwing their largesse to themselves.

Angelito turned and looked eagerly among the
fluttering boxes for Socorro. After a moment he
saw her, her face glowing, still clapping her gloved
hands. Presently he caught her eye. She pointed
vehemently at Juan Leon and waved her handkerchief.

When the great Spanish artist came back with
his quick cat-like steps to rejoin his fellow per-

former, Angelito seized his hands, then put an arm about him and kissed his cheek. This overture drew more applause.

After this Juan Leon dispatched two more bulls with the same silken technique. The fourth bull was given over to Angelito.

Chapter 19

A FEELING of the importance, of the gravity, of his coming fight filled Angelito as he listened to the heraldic bugle and watched the fourth bull make its dramatic entrance into the arena. It was a splendid red animal, and as he studied its swift charges in the preliminary *banderilla* play he could hear the American and the Venezuelan still conversing in the box behind him.

Presently the simple opening play was finished and now the *banderilleros* were pinning the bull with short brightly colored lances stuck in pairs atop the rolling shoulder muscles.

The thought that he must advertise himself in this momentous fight pressed on Angelito's mind. His heart gradually quickened in anticipation of the coming fray. And there was another cause of excitement in Angelito, the genuine love of the sport. The sight of the satiny bull thrilled him with the delight a player takes in a perfect instrument. The thoroughbred bull was perhaps a third faster than the creole bulls Angelito had been fighting, but it had one marked factor of safety, it always charged true. It was, as the *circo* was shouting at that moment, "a noble bull." Creoles were tricksy devils; often they lunged not at the lure, but at the *torero's* body. But this red bull was a superb creature. On it he would illustrate his skill, he would spread before the world the daring that was in his heart. As he watched the play he began planning a battle worthy of such a foe. On the tide of this *corrida* he would sail into the *circos* of Spain.

As these grandiloquent thoughts paraded through his head, he had that peculiar feeling of being observed. He glanced around and caught the eyes of Socorro Jiminez looking intently at him. Her face was white. She shook her head and made a negative sign with her forefinger.

Angelito saw that she was terrified for his safety. He thought how little she knew of the glory that was dawning for her. He smiled gloriously at her, entranced by the vision of their future career together.

The *banderilleros* were now through with their overture and the bull had come to a splenetic stand on the sunshot *"sol"* side of the arena. Three pairs of gay lances hung from its bleeding shoulders. A *monosabio* named Filipe came running around the barriers with rapiers and offered them for Angelito's selection. He chose one he had used oftener than any of the others. It was a fine blade with a yellowed ivory handle. It had been given him by an old amateur on his third bullfight after he had come out of the Matadero. That was a fight up on the Orinoco in Cuidad Bolivar. When he had finished an old *novillero* had come up, made a handsome speech and presented him this sword. He still recalled phrases of what the old man had said: "Invincible courage . . . immortal fame . . . Mars of the bullfighting world . . ." That had been four years ago. Now he was a principal in one of the greatest *representaciós* that ever came to Venezuela. The old man's prediction was coming true.

As Angelito chose this weapon he made a certain gesture to another *monosabio*. The lad turned and went flying behind the barrier to a door that let into a store room under the boxes. Presently he returned bringing with him an ordinary stout chair.

The whole amphitheater watched intently as the bright green figure approached the bull with the chair in one hand and his cape and sword in the other. The chair piqued the curiosity of the crowd;

such a homely implement brought a faint sense of bathos into the drama. A voice shouted "Milking time!" Came a ripple of the laughter of buffoons.

It was slight, but it angered Angelito in his wrought-up state. He thought savagely, "They will see! They will see!"

The bull glared at Angelito as he placed the chair on the sand in front of it. The animal seemed trying to fathom what new attack and torture this manœuver foreshadowed.

Quite deliberately, the *torero* sat in the chair, leaned back, crossed his legs in the most indolent attitude, but every instant he was taut, ready to whip aside from danger. Still leaning back, balanced on the hind posts of his chair, the fighter whipped his cape and sword at the bull.

Instantly the red monster charged. Came a blur of action, a sort of massive prestidigitation. The chair flew high in air. The green figure was seen standing just to one side of the bull's furious follow-through.

Angelito thrilled to this intimate grazing of destruction. The animal-scented aura of the bull enveloped him. The brute wheeled. Simultaneously he gauged the distance of the whirling bull and watched the fall of the chair. It fell, turning over and over. He watched it with the concentration of a juggler. He reached up his free arm, caught and controlled its whirl, brought it down on the sand and sat in it so nearly simultaneously that it gave a fantastic impression that he had never budged from his position, but had dropped out of the air firmly seated in the chair.

Laughter and applause filled the cheap *"sol"* section of the amphitheater. They broke into a roar of applause when the great red bull charged a second time, tossed the chair again, and a second time Angelito caught it and instantly resumed his seat.

This extraordinary feat was performed in swift succession four or five times in the growing uproar of the audience.

"Bravos" and *"Oles"* roared out of the poorer half of the *circo*. Sombreros were flung on the sand. The *hoi polloi* howled ecstatically at this exhibition of acrobatic skill. Here and there in the *"sombra"* side a few hands clapped. This queer division of the amphitheater into "hot" and "cold" registered on Angelito and stung him. From the artistocratic half came calls, "Juggler! Acrobat!"

He was a juggler and an acrobat because his exhibition of muscular skill was treading on the heels of an extraordinary esthetic spectacle. But the peon in the ring had no hint of this stultifying sequence. A kind of fury to succeed tingled through him. Somehow he was not grasping his immense opportunity. He was losing half, the more consequential half of the *circo*. He flung himself more recklessly into his play. The bull retorted with a fury equal to his own. The huge animal plunged beneath his outstretched arms, wheeled to charge again. Angelito placed his cape behind his back and offered his lithe body as a target for the needle horns. The creature lunged; the fighter slewed aside. The bull flashed past in a whirl of hot rank air and flung up the red silk behind the *torero*. It was the same sort of razor-edged, uncomfortable performance as the knife-thrower in vaudeville.

The *"sol"* section, filled with peons, was boiling with applause. This jugglery, this grazing of destruction was of their very ilk and stripe. This daredevil fighter was playing with a Spanish bull exactly as he would toy with a young bull.

Such continued one-sided applause loosed a regular fury of recklessness in the athlete. At the next charge of the red beauty, the *torero* whirled, laid a hand on the broad red back among the *banderillas* and sprinted over the sand by the creature's side. The brute whirled and tried to reach him.

The man whirled with it. Bull and man became involved in a spinning circle; red, with a green center. The whole was a blur, a dizzy gyration.

Even the aristocratic *"sombra"* broke into an uproar at this terrible spinning. A thousand voices broke out: *"Ole! Bravo! Magnifico!* What a man! *Ole! Bravo! Bravo!"*

In the boxes even the American visitor was lifted to his feet: "Go it, baby! I'm for yeh, though I don't see how the hell you'll ever get out o' there!"

To Angelito the amphitheater was revolving in a blur of color. Suddenly reversing his straining muscles he flung himself out of the votex, past the bull's tail. The fighter checked the dizzy swing of his eyes and stood poised and facing the animal. The din of the spectators shook his ears.

He had meant now to kill the animal, but he was just capturing the aristocrats and this universal pandemonium spurred him on to a last *tour de force.* He would overwhelm the amphitheater.

As the bull charged again he ran backwards toward the *"sombra"* side. He was aware when he passed out of the slanting sunshine into the shadow. He saw the long blue shadow sweep over the furious bull as it came at him head down. This time Angelito did not lure the bull to one side with his cape. He stood tiptoe, one foot a little in advance of the other as though he meant to sprint at the bull.

As the huge red brute hurtled in, Angelito caught an impression of the short red bristles at the base of the horns; the terrific bulge of the red neck, the swinging *banderillas* . . . now it was on him . . . the *espada* placed one foot between the bull's horns, and, with the terrific up-toss, leaped . . .

The whole amphitheater gasped, thundered in applause. Angelito's daring had peonized even the critical taste of *"sombra."* He had bludgeoned them into a crude primitive worship of rashness and peril; he had effaced the cool aristocratic universe of ideal beauty. He had won.

With the tremendous heave of the bull's head, Angelito felt himself rise in air, glimpsed the broad red back of the bull flashing under him. But amid the terrific strain he felt a hot tearing pain in his side where Señor Montauban had thrust. This exquisite agony destroyed the cat-like poise that would have dropped him on his feet again. The yellow sand swung up, struck him a trifle sidewise, his feet tripped, he fell heavily.

In his pain, Angelito saw the bull whirl and lunge back at him. Beyond the bull came the

bright figures of Juan Leon and the *banderilleros*
dashing toward him. But the bull was upon him
again. He tried desperately to roll out of its way.
The down-thrust head and sharp black horns were
right over him . . . the smell of an animal . . .
the whole universe shaking about him shot through
with profound pain. He felt himself lifted. The
amphitheater seemed to swing up and down, into
the sunshine, into the shadow, the sunshine, the
shadow . . . the bull had tossed him twice.

The American spectator was getting out of his
box with shaking legs and a chalky face. His
Venezuelan companion was begging him to stay, the
fight would go on, the bull, and two others, would
be killed. . . .

A box party of Venezuelans and a gentleman
from the press box also were hurriedly leaving the
bullfight. They entered a large motor outside and
drove rapidly in the direction of Paraiso.

A little later from behind the gloomy red pile of
the *circo* rattled an ambulance clanging a bell for
the crowd in the plaza to make way. An old peon
woman with a sheaf of lottery tickets came stum-
bling after the clanging vehicle screaming, *"Mi hijo!
Mi hijo!"*

The crowd in the plaza were poor people who

had not enough money to see the fight. Now they
stared after the rattling ambulance and after the
old woman, and they told each other with widened
eyes that one of the *toreros* had been killed or
wounded. . . . "God's lightning, and me outside!"
They cursed their luck with great bitterness.

Presently a renewed tumult boiled up in the enormous red bowl, the *sans culotte* drew close again
and listened more feverishly than ever as the fight
went on.

Epilog

THE Señora Jiminez insisted with a masterly mass-
ing of arguments that her daughter, Socorro Jiminez, should not accompany the funeral procession
to the cemetery. Socorro was physically unfit for
the exertion; there was no need stressing the fact
of her recent engagement; the whole affair had
been somewhat veiled, and so, considering everything, it would be best not to go. Certainly Socorro would remain her six months in mourning—
black was very becoming to the girl—and of course
poor Narciso could come around occasionally to
cheer her up. There could be nothing inappropriate in that when one considered everything.

In point of fact, the funeral procession was very
small, and, as the Señora afterwards pointed out
when she heard her son's description of it, it would
never have done for Socorro to be seen in such a
paltry group. So she had been right after all.

Services for the dead fighter were held in the
Church of the Candelaria and here were gathered
a number of peons from the neighborhood of

Traposo *calle*. But old Ana declined to hire car-
riages and, after all, no crowd of Venezuelans can
walk.

The cortege that went to the cemetery was the
hearse, old Ana and Rafael in a cab, and behind
them came some little boys who had found out that
the dead man had been a bullfighter, and with the
fealty of boys to their heroes, they made the long,
hot march through the sunshine in his procession.

The cemetery in Caracas is a large enclosure
with fine tombs and carefully kept burial plots in
the foreground. But, in the manner of all things
Venezuelan, its after part is weed-grown and un-
kempt. The walls around this after part are thick
and high, and are, in reality, long tiers of vaults
for the reception of the poverty-stricken dead. In
these vaults are sealed up the poor for so long a
space of time as the family can or will pay the rent,
then the bones are taken out and thrown into a
ditch among the weeds at the back of the burial
ground.

Old Ana rented one of these vaults for her son
even as she had rented one, years ago, for her husband. In the mortuary chapel at the entrance of
the cemetery the last services were held for the
dead bullfighter. In this chapel the body lay in

state in a magnificent syp coffin, but this coffin, too, was rented for the ceremony, and a little later the cadaver was transferred to a very cheap plain box and was placed in one of the vaults in the wall. All this old Ana did neither cynically nor unlovingly, but with the utmost grief and affection. It was the custom of peons.

Rafael Jiminez was the only aristocrat at the burial. He stood for a long time watching the old woman as she knelt, sobbing among the weeds that skirted the vaults. The hot sunshine fell over wall and weeds and weeping old woman. The ditch in which all the bones were finally flung exhaled a noisome and penetrating odor that reminded Rafael of the bullring. Toward the front of the cemetery arose the marbled and flowered tombs of the aristocrats.

The poet's thoughts flowed on and on in a sad, wistful reverie. The handsome tombs spoke to him of the incurable vanity of his class, it reacted on himself and shamed his endless making of verses.

This futile, foolish aristocracy had been the one goal of Angelito's life, but into it he had never crossed. However, he had succeeded in one thing. Rafael knew his sister would never cease to love the man they were laying to rest to-day in this cheap vault of the poor. The only power that could ever have shaken Socorro's passion for the bullfighter was Angelito himself, and now his hands were stilled.

In time to come he knew that Socorro would marry Narciso Montauban, as he himself eventually would marry Margherita Miraflores. . . .

Pues, it was all very well . . . she whom he had so long and so barrenly desired, that exquisite, understanding, and passionate woman, whom the fancy of his adolescence had endlessly painted, she either could not be found or was not at all.

But his sister, Socorro, had known the man who had moved her to the very foundation of her being; a glimpse had been vouchsafed her; evanescent it was, and its continuance perhaps had been impossible, but at least, for her one short day, she had lived.

In his heart he was glad of that; he was thankful that this one little crumb of immortality had dropped into his sister's lap from the banquet of the indifferent gods.

THE END